# SOMEBODY KEEPS CALLIN'

# Somebody Keeps Callin'

## D. Harrigon

Copyright © 2024 by David Dawkins
All rights reserved. No part of this book may be reproduced in any manner whatsoever without written permission except in the case of brief quotations embodied in critical articles and reviews.
First Printing, 2024

With grateful thanks to Asa Gim Palomera
for all her support

**Content Warning**
Descriptions of gore and body horror.
Mentions of rape culture and trafficking.

# Contents

Dedication — v

| | | |
|---|---|---|
| 1 | Cottage | 1 |
| 2 | Roads | 17 |
| 3 | Suburbs | 33 |
| 4 | Village | 45 |
| 5 | Studio | 57 |
| 6 | Countryside | 73 |
| 7 | Interior | 93 |
| 8 | Car | 109 |
| 9 | Headquarters | 125 |
| 10 | Bed | 143 |
| 11 | Factory | 155 |
| 12 | Quarry | 171 |
| 13 | Inn | 185 |
| 14 | Church | 197 |
| 15 | Mansion | 209 |
| 16 | Estate | 227 |

**VIII** |

*Acknowledgements* 233

# 1

# Cottage

I wake up, tongue thick and awkward in my dry mouth, eyes sticking shut. There's almost a sound, like a little '*plep*,' as I open them and see the headless body lying next to me.

Oh, no. Not again.

Just. Fucking. Brilliant.

Tears sting my eyes. Bile rises in my throat. Dry swallow.

Every time. I can't take this any more. I can't get used to this. I just can't. Whatever it is that allows people to become inured to such things is broken in me. Another piece that's missing.

His spine spills from his torso like some lolling tongue, covered in sinew and gore. I close my eyes again so I don't have to look at… Headless. Yeah. Let's call him Headless. It's always best if you don't remember their names.

I was having a weird dream. I try to remember it, because my dreams are meaningful and are often trying to tell me something. More so than yours.

Focus.

Do I even have time to dig a hole? And with what? My bare hands?

Fuck!

When did my life get so fucked up that my first reaction to waking up next to a headless corpse is, 'Do I have time to dig a hole?' rather than, 'Aaaaahhhh! Dead body!'

Focus.

My dream. Something about trees. A tall pine forest, but really tall pines. The kind you don't get here in England.

Perhaps it's a memory from my travels.

More likely something I saw in a movie.

The swaying giants surrounded a little log cabin. One of those American cabin-in-the-woods deals, but old and so, so small. I don't recognise it, but it was hiding something.

In the dream, I was searching, forever hunting, something close-up and also very far away. The giant trees were my fingers, sunk deep into the earth. I tried to lift my hands. The whole clearing, with the cabin and the track and everything, lifted towards my head, which was the sun, roiling and burning. My light blasted into the windows, desperately trying to see, to find. Everything was too bright. Smouldering. Too hot, too intense. It all started burning.

No, no good. It's faded.

What was I looking for?

Shifting my position on the mulch, one hand groping at the twig sticking into my boob, I try to- Wait, what? I'm lying on dirt?

Ah, shit.

My eyes crack open once more, I deliberately force them shut. Not again. Please, no. Not again. I don't want to see. Don't want to know.

Too late. I can smell it now, the scent of a forest. That sharpness of the organic in my nostrils. I'm not just dreaming about forests, I'm in a fucking forest.

You know what this is like? I know exactly what this is like. You throw a party and have a bunch of friends over, you're all drunk, the neighbours have told you at least twice to keep the noise down, then your phone wakes you up way too early the next morning, and you look at it with your head pounding, and it's your boss who says you have to come into work today.

Bullshit, is what it is.

I'm on a gentle hillside in a messy woodland of half-arsed beech and hawthorn. Straggling, unphotogenic under-brush. The path leads to this wider, flatter section then trails away deeper into the woods. The ground holds scant patches of grass, wild vines, mostly a mulch of forest detritus. Thin cloud cover dims the half-moon. Most of my surroundings are lost in the cool darkness.

A deeper shiver runs through me. I'm not dressed for this.

Fuck a troll. Why does this keep happening to me? But I know why.

I know what kind of girl I am.

The chill and my disappointment in myself is enough to drag me to my knees. Late One Summer's Night. Or is it early one late-spring morning? I need my phone to check the date. Where's my phone? Oh, right. In my handbag.

Which is nowhere I can see!

I hug myself and rub my arms, rub my chest, getting a bit of warmth back. My chest is damp with something dark and sticky. Blood. Lovely. Ruined my blouse, soaked into my bra. Fortunately, the tape under my ribs is still secure.

Years and years of this shit. But, for some fucked-up reason, I can't stop.

How long do I have?

Was Headless taking me somewhere to hold himself, or delivering me to people who'll be missing him? My little sleeps are brief enough, but five minutes can be an age if you're waiting for someone to turn up with a new girl.

I squint through my blonde fringe, groggily searching for a cup of water. I usually put out some water. I get dehydrated after one of my episodes. But this is a fucking FOREST so no glasses, cups, goblets, pitchers, mugs, chalices, tumblers or even the holy fucking grail, to be seen anywhere. No water. I have a bottle in my bag. If I can find my bag.

Wait. Blonde? I'm not fucking blonde! Oh. A wig. Part of my disguise. Fixed nice and firm, so I leave it.

Let's deal with the elephant in the clearing, shall we?

Smaller build. He seems short. I'm a hundred and seventy-six centimetres. Yes, I was raised in Australia and think in centimetres, you Imperial-measurement-using throwbacks. Okay. Fine. Around five-eight, five-nine in the old measurements.

I can't be sure how tall he was until I find his head.

Jeans. A sweater not a hoodie, a nice coat, but no jewellery, not even a watch. Might not be much of haul from this one, then. It's not like I do it for the money, but that does help. Hopefully he has a nice, fat wallet.

I pulse to my feet in one long, graceful movement. Pity there's no one around to see it. Stretching, I dust off the mulch and try to wipe off some of the blood. None of it's mine, obviously. Did I toss my handbag into the trees? Leave it behind me, down one of these tracks?

My jacket is nearby. An ugly green thing with black, faux-leather arms. Do you remember that horrible trend? That's what I get for diving through charity dumpsters. A hint of my body warmth lingers as I slip it back on. Better.

No bag. Anywhere. I'm dressed, boots and all, but my blouse is torn and a button is missing. That explains the dead body. I can guess what the fucker was up to. Was Headless sampling the goods or did I just pick a wrong 'un?

Shit. What month is this?

Ah, fuck it! I hate waking up like this! I hate it! Why do I keep doing this to myself?

Where's my damned bag? I should find that. Tears keep leaking into my eyes, I don't even know what fucking day it is, how the fuck am I expected to deal with a corpse?

No.

Focus. I might not have long, so I need to-

Oh, shit. Hairs! Dammit! If they find one stray hair I am fucked! I crouch, scratching at the mulch, hands shaking from the cold. Forensics are viciously effective nowadays. I know they have my fingerprints on file. I don't want to give them a strand of my hair for their- No, wait. I'm wearing a FUCKING WIG! For fucks' sake!

I am an idiot.

I don't know if they have my DNA, but I really don't want to give them a random sample. Fucking cops.

The corpse is lying there. Insolently. This is the bit of my life that's less fun. Could I just...?

My chest sinks, head dropping back. With a growl of frustration that would impress a passing lioness, I stomp over.

The initial tear point was on the left. His left. O! but there's a lot of blood. Some of it spurted. The skin and muscles are jagged. Torn, not cut. The beast was enraged. Probably tossed the head in the same direction as the tear. Down the slope.

I can't see it. Can't tell if that was before or after his chest was wrenched open, a jagged lining of broken ribs and the whole sternum hinged out to one side, leaving a bloodied maw in his torso.

It's kind of my signature.

There's probably a lone detective with a file of connections he can't convince anyone is worth pursuing. The walls of his office are covered in photos, notes and sketches, linked together with different coloured threads. "Look! All the bodies have the same injury! Chest torn open! Why won't you believe me?"

I pick up a sturdy twig and have a little poke about in the cavity. The thick lungs resist my stick like a damp face-cloth. Bile rises again and I lean back, staring up at the dark sky. A few settling breaths and I'm not going to throw up. I need some water. Fuck, I hate this part. It should get easier but it never does. His heart is still there, so at least I don't have to go looking for that.

The shrill sound of a nasty little pop song screams into the night.

Oh.

Fuck.

That's his phone.

Someone's missing him.

It's in the back pocket of his jeans, muffled, but way too loud in the night. I tuck my stick into an inside pocket. Can't leave that lying around now I've touched it. Rolling Headless over, the song screeches louder until I find the volume button and thumb it all the way down.

I peer into the woods.

Nothing.

The screen shows no fucking name associated with the number. Why is my life never that simple?

The trail behind is all churned up. Obviously, I did my best thrashing-about routine to mark up the ground, make it easier for me to find my way back. That's something Hansel and Gretel never tried, dragging each other through the woods while they thrashed about. Way better than breadcrumbs.

His destination was that way, then. Nothing along there that I can see. No-one coming. How long will that last? The screen shows no missed texts.

How much time do I have?

Who exactly is this guy? I can't remember. Damn. My notebook will have the relevant scribbles. I hate looking at the writing I do when I'm... Not me. I know my own handwriting. That's not my handwriting.

First I have to find my handbag.

No time!

Are there other people waiting, or was he supposed to call and confirm? Back that way is my stolen car, or his car, or van? I kind of feel like we came in his car.

Perhaps that's where my handbag is.

What's farther along the path? I go through all this shit for information, so a quick run along the track seems useful. Besides, it'll warm me the fuck up.

No bag, no head, no clue.

Damn, but my brain is busy. I can't settle, pick a thread. Don't you just hate it when you get a whole bunch of information dumped on you randomly. It's like when you pick up a book and the story starts in the middle without giving you any background or context. You have to infer everything from details and just hope it will all eventually make sense.

Rising, I button my jacket over my bloodied blouse, staining the lining. Doesn't matter. I can burn them without getting all sentimental. Try and rescue one favourite, blood-stained t-shirt and it can nearly get you busted.

Procedures. If you do something often enough you work out procedures. Months of looking up stuff in the library, on the internet, chatting up policemen. I make solid plans. Okay, you can laugh at that. You know what they say about the best laid plans of mice and murderers.

I roll Headless to the edge of the clearing. Fuck the head. The foxes can have it.

The main trail is level enough for a run. My feet pound quietly in the dirt as I warm up and wake up. There's nothing immediately apparent, though darkness and the twists of the under-used track make it difficult to see too far ahead. I pick up the pace, breathing stronger. Why? Why is my blood thumping in my ears? I would go insane if I thought too deeply about it. The breeze rustles the forest about me, covering a degree of noise.

After a hundred metres or so, to the left, downhill, I spy something. A line through the forest. Ah. Wire fencing. Tall and intended to keep out visitors. The masking evergreens planted on the other side press up against the chain-link like they're trying to escape a horrific fate. A side-track leads vaguely down in that direction. I follow it.

After running along the edge of the fence for fifty metres or so, a tall, metal-framed, wire gate huffs into view, with a 'No-Trespassing' sign.

English. So, I'm still in England. Or somewhere in the UK. Or, at least, somewhere the signs are written in English. I'm not going to tell you about that time I woke up in fucking Hungary; we'd be here all night.

The gate is locked, looming higher than I can reach. I'm not short. A hundred and seventy-six- Wait, I said that already. Pain will help. Back-heeling myself in the shins, the stinging rises, causing sparks. Oh, but that feels so good.

Yeah, so, pain does feel bad to me, but mostly it fills me with... Well.

I jump over the gate, crouching to absorb the sound as I thump down from on high. My ankles tingle from the landing. My dodgy knee strains but doesn't complain overmuch. I feel the beast dancing at the sensations. Focus. No time for that. Carefully, I make my way down the path.

There's a light ahead. Above a back door.

It's a horribly old cottage in a terrible state of disrepair. One room. Thick moss covers the tiles, though a couple look newer. Not exactly a log cabin. England doesn't do those. This is some old woodsman's cottage. There's probably no water connected to this land, which is why it hasn't been turned into a country-commuter mansion or six. The faint hum of a generator running in that dilapidated lean-to tells me it's not even hooked up to the electric. I'd bet money the sink inside has a hand pump.

This is the kind of place a weird old uncle might live, hiding in the woods, all alone, with stacks of mouldy magazines and a collection of broken memories.

Only, Headless wasn't alone.

Someone else is moving inside.

The interior is brighter than the half-moon night. There's definitely a shape in there, behind the curtains. Male? Female? More than one? Can't tell.

The fact that the generator is barely audible speaks of something modern and probably expensive. Suspicious.

This whole place needs investigating. But not now. I don't have all my stuff so I can't get any decent information. The occupants are not relaxed and over-sharing. They're waiting for their man to arrive, and he hasn't. Everyone inside will be on high alert by now. My identity would be too easily compromised, wig and all. Then there's Headless to deal with.

May. I remember, now. It's the middle of May. That makes it around half-three in the morning. I got his contact from a prostitution ring I uncovered by following that suspicious cop on his day off, when he went to get his freebie.

Clunk goes the latch. The back door opens a creaking crack. A tall man emerges muttering something into a mobile. He pulls the dark rectangle from his ear and begins that irregular tapping that signifies calling someone on his contacts list.

Shit! He's going to head out and look for Headless!

The black polo-shirt and brown, waxed jacket mark him as some ex-army type. The effect is exacerbated by a buzz-cut, a thick, strong body that moves with ease and confidence, a heavy brow, but bright, intelligent eyes shining in the glow from the screen.

Quickly, quietly, like a fox when the farmer comes, I scamper back to the gate. Panic and fear give me more than enough to jump back over, landing relatively silently on the other side. His phone torch waves towards me from the house, behind the treeline. Doesn't matter. He won't keep up.

I bolt along the path as fast as my legs can carry me. Which is pretty fucking fast.

Cursing under my breath all the way back, my dodgy knee flicks the occasional needle into my nerves. I don't think Bright-Eyes spotted me, but if they spook, they'll abandon the cottage and that's everything lost. I'll have to start all over again.

That sinking feeling crawls into my gut. This is my life? All this bullshit? Is this all there is until the end of fucking time?

No. I'm not going to fall apart. I can get out of this. Get some information. Follow the thread and see where it leads.

Then I'll fall apart.

I hug the lower path. It's rougher and will slow Bright-Eyes down if he has spotted me. I try to gauge when I'm below the clearing, but there's no need. A pale roundness marks the corner of a narrow track leading up.

Never have I ever been so happy to see a disembodied head.

It's tangled in the fucking brambles a little way from the track. Thorns and nettles ruin my already ruined outfit as I reach in. I'm far enough ahead of Bright-Eyes not to give too much of a fuck about the noise. I get a handful of dead hair. Not buzz-cut, like Bright-Eyes. Headless is not part of the gang? Have I found a link to a higher ring? The noggin is heavy. A human head weighs roughly the same as a bowling ball. I catch my balance as I haul myself upright, prize firmly gripped. Now, to get the rest of him.

The body is still in the clearing, right where I sort-of hid it. Two missed calls. I hold down the power then tap it off completely. Should have done that when I first found his fucking phone.

Procedures.

He's wearing one of those trendy, short raincoats with lots of belts. There's a belt at the waist, belts at the wrists. After I've turned up the collar, there's even a belt at the neck. I pull this taut and tie it, covering his bloody truncation, and hopefully stopping the worst of the drips.

Still no sign of Bright-Eyes. Maybe he's not even coming. Oh, wait. There's a dim, distant torchlight. An actual torch, not the light from a phone.

Well-equipped. Professional. Definitely a rung up the ladder of baddies.

I heave the body over one shoulder, pick up the head like a handbag - where is my fucking handbag? - and jog lightly back along the path, following the remnants of my thrashing and kicking. Headless isn't that heavy. Well, not for me. Relatively.

As for my handbag, there's nothing in it that can be traced to me. It'll be a pain to replace everything, and there's probably fingerprints, DNA. But unless it's covered in his blood, it's purely circumstantial. Besides, it's not going to be the fuzz investigating this. I'll just dump the body and I'm sort of clear. Oh, crap, I hope I can dump this body.

Am I near the ocean? These people usually have their bases near the sea. Shipping access.

For some reason, I get an idea of The Chilterns, which is not convenient for the ocean, but that might just be my muddled head trying to stress me out. The Chilterns is where it all started for me. In a red-tiled room, a whole bunch of people gathered around, chanting. Men in robes. That nightmare of a fucking knife. The blade all twisted and old-looking. A jewelled handle. Lurking on a cushion until the man in the big mask picked it up and-

Huh. My own private hell.

How far away is the fucking car? This is getting ridiculous. A torch following me at a slow, searching pace. Me trotting ahead with the corpse he's looking for.

Oh, Finally! Pointing straight up the trail, right at me, is a Volkswagen Jetta. Really, Headless? A Jetta? And an old Jetta. Ah, no sat-nav, so the car is not inherently traceable.

My bag! My bag's on the back seat! A nice, big, purple Mandarina Duck. Oh, thank fuck for that.

The boot is locked. I dump Headless onto the stony track, drop his top beside, and catch my breath. The glow moves through the woods but it's way too far away for me to see a hint of the torch.

Quickly, now.

The keys are in his trouser pocket. I think I brushed against his dick when I fished them out. Absently rubbing my hand against my bloodied coat, I peer through the window. What? I'm just going to open the boot without checking if the alarm is on? That's not a mistake I'll make twice.

It's off.

I unlock the trunk. With the key, not a button on the fob, so the lights don't flash.

The head drops in with a distinctive thunk, and I roll the body after it.

The car is angled up the hill. If I just let off the hand-brake it should roll back without me having to start the engine, all noisy because it's not electric. The track gets steeper before it gets shallower, going around a dog-leg. I am shit at steering backwards. What the hell is the proper name for that? Reversing. I'm so bad at reversing I can't even think of the right word.

Okay. The shaking is more or less under control. Won't have to look at the horror in the boot until I dump it. Didn't throw up. And I found my handbag! It may surprise you to hear, I've had far worse nights.

Should not have said that.

I gently lower the boot-lid, let it half-click into place before pressing down and sealing the steel sarcophagus, quiet as I can be. There's a slight clunk as the door opens, not even locked, then the interior light comes on. Damn. I slip in quickly and gently pull the door, reaching up to click it off. Hopefully, Bright-Eyes is too far away to notice that. Maybe.

The key slides into the ignition. A manual transmission. Great. I drop the gear lever into neutral, release the handbrake.

Nothing.

The car doesn't move at all.

Fuck.

The torch is creeping closer.

I rock in the seat a little. Then a little more.

Still nothing.

Fuck. My. Life.

Maybe the car's caught on a rock? I open the door a crack, jamming one foot onto the ground, trying to get some traction, shifting my position in the seat to-

"Oi!"

Ah shit. It's Bright-Eyes. Clever bastard dimmed his torch to preserve his night-vision, that's why I thought he was farther away.

The light from his torch makes me flinch, covering my eyes as it flicks up on full. It's not bright enough for him to see me properly at this distance but he's already running closer. Close enough and he'll get a good look at me. There's something I can do about that.

I pull my leg back inside, slam the door and gun the engine, flicking the headlights on to high-beam. Bright-Eyes flinches in turn, arm up, stumbling to a stop. So much for his night vision.

I rev up and drop her into reverse. The Jetta lurches over some minor obstacle and immediately swerves to one side. I twist the steering the wrong way and then violently the other way.

I hate going backwards!

Bright-Eyes is running again, pounding down the track, squinting, like a Terminator that's forgotten its glasses. I'm too incompetent to floor it. I ease round the dog-leg, starting to leave him behind in spite of my timidity. He can't run as fast as he'd like, headlight-blinded on uneven ground. There's a longer stretch, allowing me a little more speed, with the odd puddle to test my nerve and the car's suspension.

I glance back and Bright-Eyes is still running. Does he think he can outrun a fucking car? Then I ease around the last corner and the answer becomes obvious.

There's a gate! There's a fucking gate! I jam on the brakes, yank the handbrake, and almost fall out of the car in haste. Which promptly stalls because I forgot to take it out of gear. Shit. Fucking manual transmission!

I race down. There's a chain and padlock, but it's not fastened. Headless didn't plan on being up the lane for long. I flick off the latch and yank hard. The gate swings inwards. I braked soon enough that the car doesn't prevent me from opening it. I can hear the pounding of running feet. Closer. Closer. I slip into the car, and glance up. Bright-Eyes is nearly at the corner of the track. Accelerating. And grinning.

He's still squinting, so I don't think he's seen me clearly. The wig will help with that. Lucky I kept it on.

Panic shoots ice into my nerves. I almost freeze.

A deep breath and I flick the Jetta out of gear, gun the engine. It doesn't start but then it does and I almost fumble the gearstick trying to get it into reverse.

Handbrake! Oh, fuck!

Bright-Eyes is at the bonnet, making his way along the overgrown verge down to my door. I keep my face turned away. The Jetta lurches into motion. He stumbles. I practically spin out into the narrow, country lane, kicking the clutch, fishing for first before the car has even stopped.

Bright-Eyes comes rushing up, reaching for the door. The Jetta lurches forward and he misses the handle. His weight slams into the car, rocking it violently. Big guy. I accelerate away, rolling him off onto the tarmac. He climbs to his feet and flings the torch at the car in frustration.

Second gear.

There's a clunk as the torch bounces off harmlessly, and I leave him in my dust.

That got my pulse pounding. How does that happen? Why is there a loud rhythm of panic in my ears? A flush of adrenalin? How does all that even work?

Third gear.

Okay. Now. I'm driving down an unknown country lane, in a stolen car, in the trunk of which is the head and body of a man too cheap to spring for SatNav, and I may have just blown my only lead.

Like I said, I've had worse nights.

I glance in my rear-view. Bright-Eyes is a vanishing dot. Still running. How does he think he's going to catch me, now? Wait. What's he doing with his hand? Oh, he's making a phone call! Fuck! I hate those fucking mobiles! The idea of them is so foreign. Call anyone from anywhere, anytime. Annoying little things.

I pass a gated opening on my right, roughly far enough along for it to be the entrance to a track that leads up to the front of the dilapidated cottage.

There'll be a noise, so I roll down the window, a blast of cool air on my face, and quite possibly the faint sound of an engine starting in my ears. Distant headlights flick on.

Shit.

Why is it never easy to rip off someone's head and dump their body?

No mistaking that noise. The crack and pop of tires on a rough road, with the throaty roar of a diesel engine underneath. They have another car.

There's going to be a chase.

# 2

# Roads

Darkness rushes into the car as I kill the headlights. The lane is a proper, winding country road, following the base of the hills. High hedgerows, close on either side, hide whatever is around each treacherous corner. Dangerous to drive down on a half-lit night without lights.

I don't slow. It doesn't matter if I scratch the paintwork. It's not my car.

Their car is probably faster than this. The Jetta is sluggish pulling away from the corners, the steering heavy through them. Headless was so cheap, he bought a low-powered petrol engine version. Probably quieter than the diesel, which is something. When you've stolen as many cars as I have, you get snobbish with it.

Oh, here they come. Roaring, blasting their high-beams into the night.

A high-speed chase through rural England.

Nah, fuck that.

There's a junction ahead, another lane leading down to the left. With all the twists, I don't get much warning. I dump off the power, but don't touch the brakes. No red brake-lights for you, Bright-Eyes.

Not enough.

I drop down a couple of gears and the engine over revs, way too loud a noise and still not slowing me enough. I make a split second decision, tap the brakes, lighting the hedgerows red, then accelerate along the road I'm on, ignoring the turning.

I make it to the next bend and they're not in my rear-view. Can't tell if they fell for it and turned. Woah! Shit. Nearly went into a ditch. The car judders along the embankment then plops down onto the road. So close to the ditch. I need to pay attention to my driving.

The sooner I find a bolt-hole, the better.

I'm searching for something specific as I run up to the outskirts of the village beneath the hill. Here we go. Finally, some houses coming up on the left. That's well over a mile from the cottage. Wow. Remote.

I need a house with high hedges, a longer driveway. There! That one. The wooden sign on the gate-post reads: 'Ferny Hoolet'. Unbelievable. Without touching the brakes, I gear down. No handbrake.

Door open. One jump and I'm at the gate, flick the latch, shove, jump. I slip into the driver's seat before the car comes to a completely stop. A sharp turn of the wheel and it's a gentle roll down the sloping drive.

There's a distant squeal of tires, an engine roars. My head twitches, trying to locate the source. Sound does carry at night. Lights swing around. Their diesel is too bass and low for me to tell if it's coming in this direction.

Until it starts getting louder and louder.

I curl around beside the hatchback that's already down here and kill the engine. Handbrake. Suddenly, headlights glare along the hedgerows. I curl down, peering out beneath the headrest. A huge, black Range Rover roars by, three people inside. I'm pretty sure the one in the back is Bright-Eyes, hand over his mouth in concentration.

I resist the urge to duck. The human eye reacts to movement, so staying still is more important when hiding. The huge four-by-four is going so fast they don't have time to pick me out. They probably think I'm scared, so I'll be running, trying to get away from scary them.

I'm not scared. Not in the way they think.

Plates! Ah, shit! I should have got a look at the licence plates. That might have sped things up. I snort in frustration. I'll make a note of the Jetta's tags, at least, but I'm not sure how closely Headless is associated with Bright-Eyes and the Range Rover gang.

The Range Rover Gang. A good name for a band.

Right. Let's get organised. I grab my handbag. So happy I found it! My phone? No, water first. I suck down half the damned bottle. Ooo, that's better. I drop it back into the bag along with the usual junk: purse with fake ID, tampons, a small bottle of vodka, lippy, kid-skin gloves, breath mints, compact, multi-tool, one of those big, silk scarves with that posh rope-and-anchor pattern, half-width roll of duct tape, two pens, notebook and a propelling pencil. Hidden in the lining: a taser, strike-anywhere matches, a small flask of lighter-fluid, half a dozen cable-tie handcuffs, my FN-FiveseveN automatic pistol with a Streamlight TLR-4 Tac-light/laser, extra magazine, locksmith tools, a four-pack of airtags, and my private notebook.

That last item will have the clues I need to work out how far along I am. It'll come back quicker if I read my notes. Because of my condition, sometimes it doesn't come back at all. I'll forget important details. Writing everything down is vital, but it's a massive clue to anyone who finds it. I write in code and nonsense, but that won't stop a determined mind for long.

Did you like the bit where I named the gun, with all the numbers and letters? Does that make me sound all professional and stuff? Honestly, I'm just copying it out of the catalogue.

Wait.

Bright-Eyes wasn't covering his mouth. He was talking on headphones, holding the speaker on the wire up to his mouth for clarity. He was calling another car!

How many fucking cars do these people have?

More importantly, what type of car is it? Another Range Rover? A Mercedes? A van? How do you hide from someone when you don't know what they look like?

They'll bring their reinforcements to the wrong location but there's so little traffic. A drone with a decent enough camera and they'll be able to monitor every road, track, and lane for miles around. I'll have to slip quietly behind, sneak my way around back lanes. Or, is that what they'll expect me to do?

Six minutes past four in the am, according to my burner phone. The GPS starts cycling in on my location. Never knock a Huawei, even if you can't pronounce it. Seriously, what an age we live in where I can get a dirt-cheap touch-phone that has GPS, all the apps, and comes in purple. I'm not a fan of pink, but anything purple, I'm your gal.

The spinning hourglass vanishes and the dot pops up on the map. The fucking Chilterns! I'm in the fucking Chilterns. Fucking shit fuck. One of those deep countryside places with names like Bryant's Bottom, Hyde End and Slad Lane. Fucking Buckinghamshire.

That's creepy. Tingle in the spine creepy. Around here is where it all started for me, in my own little red pit of hell. Maybe I'm chasing the same group. That thought brings half a grin.

No. It's unlikely they're still going after all these years.

Focus.

I have to get to another county before dumping Headless. The police never talk to each other across borders.

I check the location of my stolen car, marked with a star. My other stolen car. The car I stole to go and meet Headless. Oh, look, I'll explain all that later. It's too far north to be useful. It may have been compromised. Best to leave it.

The sun will peak over the hills in a little over an hour. Water. I need a big body of water, digging will take too long. I scroll the map about seeking a suitable bit of blue.

Add in time for weighting the body, dumping the Jetta, driving down B roads, etc, and I'll be getting home around seven o'clock. Not good. Roads filling with commuter traffic. Neighbours awake and nosy.

The Marina outside Reading would be okay. I've used that once before. There are several spots where it's wooded along the side and I can slip down to the shore with my 'package'. Not ideal. It leaves a line pointing straight at my house. Plus, I don't want to fill up a family fun pool with corpses.

No choice.

Oh, shit! Past this this wiggly bit, the road straightens. Dead straight, like it's following an old Roman road. They'll be able to see I'm not ahead of them!

Fuck!

I start the car, probably waking the owners of Ferny Hoolet. I *reverse* out of the drive. The red lights are a dimmer tell-tale than headlights. Maybe they're looking ahead for me, not back. I turn in the opposite direction, making for that junction I missed. With more warning, I manage to slow without using the brakes and take it easily. No other cars in sight. Who did Bright-Eyes call? What car, or cars, are they driving?

I start raking my wig-hair over my face as a kind of random mask, rolling down a narrow road with who-knows-what ahead of me. After another mile, I pass a few of those outlying commuter mansions that get tacked onto the outskirts of villages these days. Nothing suitable.

I think I can hear an engine approaching from behind. Yep, definitely headlights. Barely five hundred metres. Nothing ahead, so I accelerate, reaching the village proper. I need somewhere to hide. There's a village hall down that lane.

Where would we be without satellite navigation?

I take the turn. Yep. The hall has parking along the side and at the back, out of sight. I tuck in behind a tree-lined walk way. The roar of a passing diesel, but can't see anything. Which means, they can't see me.

It might not even have been them.

I'm always amazed how many people are trundling up and down little country lanes so early. Where are they all going at four in the morning? What's so damned important?

My dad used to make us get up at ridiculous times whenever we went on holidays, trying to beat the traffic. He liked to take us to all the traditional destinations. Now he had money, he could afford a splash-out trip to Clacton-on-Sea in his new car.

Stupid little mini.

Tiny thing. No boot space for a family, so half the luggage got stacked on the seat beside me, the rest on the roof. We'd stay by the pier and do everything, visit the theatre, swim in the sea-pool. Mum would put on her best hat. Women need to wear more hats.

Proper ones that match their outfits. I miss that. Jeans and tank tops just make the place look scruffy.

Dress better, people.

Anyway, back to the car chase. A few moments to plot a route via the Marina then around Reading to the housing estates. I have to be extra devious. Maps tells me it will take an hour to get to the lakes. I'll do it in forty minutes, and that'll still be cutting it close.

Trickling back onto the road, and after a brief scratch of my itchy wig I decide to turn on the headlights. At the speeds I'll be driving, it's too dangerous without. I'm more conspicuous to everyone else with them off. Traffic will be building.

A couple of other cars to go past before I pull out. I should be able to creep by my hunters, as long as I zag when they think I should zig.

The M40's going to be a pain. It used to be you had to work out how you were going to cross rivers. Now, you have to work out how to slip across the motorways that cut through our countryside.

If they're smart, they'll figure out those bottleneck points and cover them. Fortunately, they don't actually know where I'm going, so they and whoever else Bright-Eyes called will have to cover every possible bottleneck. And it's not like I'm going to make things easy for the fuckers.

I zip out to the wonderfully named Piddington, hang a left and drive over the motorway on Bullocks Farm Lane. A large, black four-by-four sits on the hard-shoulder of the motorway. That was quick.

The four-by-four is probably not... There's a sudden flash of activity from the open driver's window. Tires squeal. Horns blare. I put my foot down, feverishly wishing the damn Jetta had a little more punch, like a modern Jetta. A modern Jetta is a great car for hauling bodies about while dodging pursuers.

Do they know where I'm going? Or did they just get lucky? Was that even them? Is there a tracker in this car? Are you paranoid if they really are out to get you?

I sacrifice obscurity for speed and more options, zipping along Fingest Lane. My route is a surprising mix of narrow stretches with high hedges and suddenly wider roads with lots of new housing.

The countryside around here is getting really built up. Back in my day, a village council would never have approved this much new building.

Traffic is light. I slow to the pace of a car casually speeding. I see, maybe, two dozen other cars in twenty minutes, and panic over every single one of them. There is no sudden squealing of tires and ring of gunfire. No sign of Bright-Eyes and Big Black.

It's quicker to go left here but the last thing I want to do is drive through fucking Henley on Thames. The poshness of the regatta makes for a lot of added security, random cameras.

Instead, I speed through Fingest, turning south just before Turville Heath, B-roading down to Bix. Hedgerows flash past, stark against the brightening east. I loop around Sonning Common to avoid a speed camera my phone tells me is along there.

Waze, bitches.

What a lovely collection of curiously named, picturesque places I would never have thought to visit, if I didn't have a headless body in the boot and a gang of pimp-killers hunting me.

I slow to the limit and drift almost sedately along the outskirts of Caversham, which is a bunch of seventies brick shit-boxes posing as a suburb of Reading. There are bus stops along here. Buses have cameras on them. I keep a watchful eye but it's still too early for the first bus.

I'm gnawing my lip about that green car that's been behind me for, like, half a mile now? I think they call that British Racing Green. Fucking ugly colour for a car. No form of transport should have to suffer that colour, even if tradition dictates- Oh, it turned off.

Nine minutes to five and I reach the Marina unmolested and, as far as I can tell, unfollowed.

Okay, that took me longer than forty minutes, but some of those back roads were tricky. I had to slow for other drivers. This car isn't exactly a Boxter.

Driver's excuses.

A yawn fights its way through my determination. My muscles ache. I'm exhausted. The sky is light already, and the sun will be up soon. My stomach squeaks and gurgles. When was the last time I ate?

I push all that down so I can check the map and- There's a spot at the top of the Marina. A separate lake where there might not be, oh, I don't know, a rowing club getting in some early morning practice.

Stick to this main road. It's practically busy; a tussle of traffic passes every few seconds. Cars are like girls going to the bathroom, they never seem to travel alone.

I turn down another narrow lane. Really getting sick of these. The automobile exists, you know? And there are a lot of cars. This idea that villages are anything other than commuter suburbs for larger towns is ridiculous. No-one who lives in a village stays there all day any-more. We need wider roads, now! Hello? Fucking winding, country-lane bullshit.

There's a yellow boom gate buried in the hedge that looks like it hasn't been used since before I was born. Well, maybe not that long. Wait, what does that sign say? 'DMA Fisheries Limited. Private Lake. No Day Passes.' Perfect! Headless can go sleep with the fishes. Maybe one day, when I'm munching on some tinned salmon on toast, I may feast upon my prey. Is it Hamlet where he talks about how a king may go a progress through the guts of a beggar? Or maybe I don't want to show I'm that literary.

What would make you like me more?

I drive a little farther down until I find a farm gate with gravel in front. Some building looms, deeper in. Maybe the fisheries office. I pull over as much as the single lane will allow and check around.

Nobody? Cool.

Barely after five o'clock. I pop the trunk, start gathering rocks and shoving them into Headless' inside and outside pockets, poking my head up every few seconds like a meerkat checking for whatever the fuck eats meerkats.

Still nobody.

His wallet has fifteen pounds cash in it. Is that it? I can't risk taking his phone, a big Samsung thingy. Phones are too trackable, even after you've pulled the SIM. No jewellery to melt down. Forget the credit card. Fuck. I spent way more than fifteen fucking pounds on petrol.

I pull out his shirt and tie it to his belt, so the torso and legs don't separate and one or the other drifts to the surface. The head is in one of my plastic bags with some rocks of its own. A couple of holes in it to help it sink. I don't have to make holes in the body to let the gasses out as it decomposes. The beast did that already.

Even thinking about that means I have to stop and breathe for a few seconds. I'm lucky I don't remember it happening.

Okay. Fine. I do up his coat, check about one last time and haul him up onto my shoulder, hooking up the plastic bag. One finger to lever the boot closed.

There are no cameras perched on stalks, a couple of cars along the main road but that's two-hundred metres out of sight. This line of poplars leads all the way down to the water, green bushes with little white flowers on them for general cover. I don't know bushes. Carrying his extra-weighted weight on my small footprint makes me unsteady. Even stepping on tufts, I still feel the ground shift and sink oddly. Last thing I want is a twisted ankle! Oh, wait. You're not going to appreciate why that's funny.

A moment or two of careful observation from the tree at the lake's edge reveals no-one. The sun lights the sky in soft shades of pink and red. The clouds pick up the colours. All is reflected in the water. Trees add shadow and definition to the horizon, dimming the distant sounds of passing cars. I'm always amazed at sunrises and sunsets. I've seen a few in my time, and they're all beautiful, and different, all over the world.

Smacking my head repeatedly against the nearest trunk- Oh, wow, that feels good. For normal people, this would be painful. And it is, but pain connects me to the beast.

That thing that revels in sensations of any kind, that gives me my power.

The feedback of agony is so exquisite that I allow a little more of the thing to slip into me, playing with that edge of losing control.

Something dull and faded jumps into clarity. A strange man at a lonely pub full of strange men. I thought I was going to meet just one. But the rest of the men are just strangers to me. The one invites me out to his Jetta, and we go for a ride.

That's what he looks like with his head attached.

I drift back to the lake but keep more than enough in me to pick up Headless and toss him a good ten or twelve metres out into the mirror blue. The head goes farther. I take a breath and return completely.

There is a hefty *ker-shplunk* as the body hits. The clothing balloons up, but I taped the cuffs, pockets and openings shut. Remember all that stuff in my handbag? Duct tape. Useful stuff. Eventually, he sinks out of sight, consigned to the depths forever like all my childhood hopes and dreams.

There are times I miss the simple girl I used to be. Not that things ever seemed simple. Drinks with the gang. Who's sleeping with who. Does the nice boy like me? Do I like him? Why did Dad smoke so much after the diagnosis? When will the next Beatles album come out? Why does that bitch at the store hate me? Will I pass my exams? Why can't I afford everything I want? I had so many plans and dreams. Then, my life was destroyed. Now, I have to worry about forensic evidence. Vehicular pursuit. How to dispose of a body.

Also, how to dispose of a car and get home in time for breakfast.

"Excuse me! Miss?"

I'm trudging out of the private lake with the graceless, flailing walk of someone who is having trouble negotiating rough ground. Some old fucker is standing at the hedged fence with his ancient dog in tow.

"Did you throw something in the lake? I'm sure I heard a splash," he asks, all self-righteous with age and a desperate desire to be needed and relevant.

Fuck. Now I'm going to have to kill him, too.

"No, no," I reply. "I was just having a piss. There were a load of fish thrashing about near the surface." Fish do that. Best I could think of at short notice. I should probably take the dog out first. A decent sized rock would do it but the ground is mostly damp grass. No rocks.

"You're not allowed in there, you know. It's private."

"And what I was doing was private, if you don't mind."

"Well, why did you have to go all the way down there? I'm sure you're dumping rubbish. That not allowed!"

"Do I look like I'm capable of throwing something that far into the lake? Look at the ripples. That's got to be," he's old, so I have to think in old measurements, "thirty feet out! Seriously!"

He's peering at me, no glasses, so I'm fairly sure I'm just an indistinct blur to his fading eyes. That'll give me a couple of extra seconds to pin him and choke him out. Break his brittle old neck. But that will look more suspicious if he's discovered. The fish will eat the bruised skin, disguising the choke, but not a broken bone, or distorted skeleton.

"Well, why did you go that far in?"

"I have to go that far in," I'm climbing over the fence, now, "so pervy old men don't stare at me while I'm doing my business. It's different for us girls, you know. We have to look out for ourselves."

"Well, I'm not- I wasn't looking at you. I heard a noise and saw you coming back up."

"Oh, no, look, I'm sorry." I deflate my deliberately puffed up attitude and go full on apologetic. You'd be amazed how often that works. "I've been up all night and I'm a bit grumpy. I'm embarrassed about being caught short. I'm sorry. There were a bunch of big fish thrashing about. I promise, I didn't throw anything in the lake."

"Well, I don't know."

Time for the big guns. I squat. "Hello there, old boy," I say, giving his dog's neck a good rub in exactly the right spot. It's not that animals like me, I've just learned how to manipulate them. The ancient beast shuffles forward and stretches for a good scratching. "He's a beautiful old thing." I don't try and guess the breed. "How old? Or is it a she?" The old mutt is trying to get excited. I think it can smell the dried blood under my jacket.

"Oh, no, a he." The old man starts losing his train of thought, enjoying the fact that someone is enjoying his ancient dog. "Thirteen and a half, now. Getting on a bit, poor thing. I keep him exercised, though."

"Well, it's a bit early for walkies, isn't it? Sun's not even up yet."

"Oh, well, I wake up so early, these days." *Yeah? Tell me about it.* "It happens when you get older. And I figure, if I'm up I may as well do something." He's talking with the rambling desperation of someone who doesn't get much human contact, any-more. "So I come down here. It's not too far for us, and I like to watch the sun come up over the Marina. The way the light reflects in the water. Even to my old eyes, it's quite beautiful. And different every morning."

Huh. That's making me glad that I probably won't have to kill him. Lonely old ramblers with poor eyesight don't tend to make reliable witnesses.

"Well, it's good weather for it," I say, deliberately picking up on his habit of saying 'well' at the beginning of sentences.

"Oh, well, yes. I come out even if it's a bit overcast, but not in the winter. My old bones-"

"Yes, well, I've got to be on my way. So sorry about before."

"Oh, no, no. Don't mention it."

"Good luck with your sunrise." I'm already heading back to the car, waving, and glimpse him raising a hand in return. The dog half shuffles after me then decides it's too much effort.

Despite the narrow lane, the farm gate helps me make a decent three-point turn. The old man stops long enough to wave me bye-bye. I nod, and head back towards Reading. And do you know what?

The sunrise is fucking beautiful.

…and now I have to pee…

# 3

# Suburbs

I pull over in a lay-by and take care of that nagging matter behind a hedge.

There's a caravan with 'Anna's Kitchen' written on the side, all shut up. Coffee would be nice but I don't want to leave a trail of sightings. This is the kind of place my dad would stop on our holiday trails. Motorways were scant back then, and neither of my parents liked travelling on them. They were both in it for the journey. And heaven help us all if Dad brought his guitar. He always wanted to start his own skiffle band, playing old Blues songs and early Beatles, Lonnie Donegan. We'd pull over into a lay-by, get out a thermos of tea and some sandwiches Mum made the night before. Vaguely warm, slightly stale.

That pretty much describes my upbringing.

Dad wanted a boy, typical story, and Mum didn't want any more children after she'd given birth to me. She told me later the whole giving-birth thing hugely traumatised her. She had flashbacks and everything. Funny how we always think of PTSD as something that only happens to soldiers. Mum was expected to get over it, no counselling, nothing. Childbirth isn't just this beautiful thing that happens. It's a life-changer. Some get addicted, some freak out. But back then, no-one even considered these things.

They barely do now.

Mum was disowned by her upper-middle class family for marrying a factory foreman. That was before I was born. After I was born, she lost all her friends and had no-one to talk to, no source of information about birth and families and such. She had no relief from her thoughts. And Dad would just sit there, playing Mississippi John Hurt, singing with a deliberate American twang, wishing, like so many youths who remembered bombs falling on their towns, that they could fly off around the world in a rock and roll band. The Fab Four. Working class boys done good.

That's how most of my childhood holidays would start, in a lay-by, with Dad sitting on the bonnet of the car, finger-picking away, Mum sipping tea and deluding herself that she was some kind of rebel. Me? Staring through a gate at fields in various states of agriculture.

Then Dad got the 'big' promotion and we moved to Australia.

The council estate near Reading has a few high-rise towers of degrading flats. I quietly circle a nicer area of badly designed housing just near there, looking for- Yep. One of those. No. That house has an alarm. Ah, there's another one, under a nice cover, so probably well cared for. And I can't see an alarm box clinging like a limpet to the building.

That might be a bit foolish this close to a council estate. Don't get me wrong. Most people are decent, wherever they live. However, when you have a higher concentration of people, you'll have a higher number of that bad element, all influencing and exacerbating each other, sucking in the not-quite-so-wicked and just plain desperate. That creates a settled culture of baddies being bad. Like that's normal. Being bad.

Same thing happens with bankers in their office towers. You get two or three feral bastards goading each other into bigger and bigger crimes, dragging everyone else down with them. Then only the nastiest get promoted. For some reason, though, there are a lot more arrests in council estates than banking districts.

A couple of streets over there's a railway yard. Fewer people peeping when I pull over and wipe down the inside of the car, even though I'm going to burn it. You'd be amazed how much forensic evidence they can recover from a fire. Then I wipe down the outside of the car, door handle, door and frame, boot latch, briefly with the rest. Inside the boot.

It's okay. It just looks like I'm cleaning it.

I don't remember how much I touched the car, before I woke in the woods. I'm always careful with my hands, keeping them from casual contact, and I wear gloves at the slightest excuse, but you never know. I glimpse people as they pass the railyard's gate. But they're walking along the pavement on the other side of the road. None of them really look.

From the building traffic, that's the main road over there, so I should head off in that direction, cut down through there.

I splash some lighter fluid. Oh, I don't smoke, by the way, so it can't possibly have been me who splashed lighter fluid all over the car interior, boot, and the open petrol cap. It catches. The fire spreads slowly. It's not like a Hollywood, *wooOOSH!* It'll take a while, and I'll be well on my way.

I so want to stick around and watch it burn.

Farewell, Jetta. With a nice, torquey diesel engine you might have been a better car. What's that Byron line? All farewells should be sudden, when forever. I don't think you can get more forever than being set on fire. Wait, am I going with the literary thing or not? Can't decide.

Back to the other house and I peek under the sheet. Nice. Cars pass semi-regularly now, but I keep my face turned from the road. Alarm lock nestled in the handlebars and two heavy chains through the back wheel. The front door to the house, however, has a single Yale.

Moron.

I slip on my kid-skin gloves. My tool takes less than three seconds to pop that thing and I step quietly inside. Motorcycle riders tend to get up later than other people because the commute doesn't take them as long. No other car in the drive, so the wife and kids probably take the bus. Shit. I hope I don't have to kill any kids this morning. I don't quite shut the door. There's a table with mail all over it, a bowl on top with keys inside, the helmet tucked underneath. What. An. Idiot. The leather biker's jacket on the coat rack is petite with pink highlights. Huh. Girl-rider. Lives alone? Still a moron. Get a deadbolt for your door, stupid girl. And an alarm. That might at least have slowed me down. The jacket might fit, but there are other coats over it. Unnecessary racket.

"Is that you, Carmie?" a woman's voice calls from above.

I freeze like a startled cat. Shit. Was I speaking out loud, or did she hear the door? Carmie? Boy or girl?

"Carmie?" A bed creaks.

I'd better answer before she gets up. I make an unintelligible positive sound, pitched midway between male and female, bordering on a "Yeah." I'm going to leave a trail of fucking bodies at this rate. Home Invasion Goes Horribly Wrong.

"Oh, you sound a bit rough, sweetie. Put the kettle on then come up here and ravish me, bitch. Oh, and get some biscuits."

That needs a response, so I make another blurred sound bordering on a feminine, "Sure." I snag the Kawasaki key chain, tuck the helmet under one arm, leave the rest.

"You're nice and early, today. We should have time for a proper cuddle."

The door gives a little creak as I open it again, and I make sure I clomp a bit into the house before slipping back.

"I'm surprised that fucking husband of yours let you out so soon, or did you just sneak off?"

I step out and mostly close the door, not wanting it to clunk, leaving the lesbian affairs of suburban Reading behind me.

Now, I've got to be fast. Carmie could actually turn up at any moment. And her upstairs isn't going to yell conversation forever without expecting an answer. Fumbling with panic at the keychain, I fob off the alarm, undo the alarm cable and both wheelchains in short order, then start pushing. A motorcycle is one of the few types of motorised transport one person can steal without making any noise.

There are people about. Most of them peer speculatively at the rising column of dark smoke a couple of streets away, ignoring me. With my head down, I shove along rapidly and turn down another street. There are people here, too. I slip on the helmet. Ugh, too tight. The engine fires eagerly. It's not too loud and I don't rev the nuts off as I pull away. With a 600cc engine, it kicks along well enough, and I mostly remember how to cycle up through the gears.

Shit, I should have grabbed the jacket.

My chest is chilled by the time I'm a couple of miles away. The rest of me isn't much warmer. This coat isn't very wind proof. No cuffs at the end of the faux-leather arms. My gloves are daywear, not biker. But it's the torso you want to keep warm.

Stupidest. Fashion. Ever.

I pull over and the first thing I do is rub myself vigorously to get the circulation going. My hands are shaking, but that's not just the cold. A deep tightness had bedded in around my belly. I can't shake the swirling feeling in my head. I hate this. Hate being like this.

My scarf is in my handbag in the helmet box on the back. I fish it out, fold it double and jam it inside the front of my coat. It's genuine silk, so it'll be warmer, even if it gets a little blood on it. I remove the wig, spend a few moments fiddling with the webbing inside the helmet, spitting curses at the stupid fucking bitch who spent hundreds of pounds on alarms and locks for her bike, and has no alarm and a shitty lock on her front door. Let that be a lesson to you all.

The helmet's a better fit, but I need the next size up.

My notebook tells me Antonio's number. I send a quick text to let him know I'm coming in with something. It'll be nice to see the old fellow. He's very reliable. I don't really have time for any other kind of people in my life. Reliable is worth its weight in Californium 252.

I'm a little off-course but I can see the road I need to be on from here.

Swinging back out, I cross over the M4 on Kirton's Farm Road. There's a blue sedan pulled over on the hard shoulder. There's plenty of traffic, now, and I'm on a motorcycle. The car doesn't move. Maybe it's a genuine breakdown.

I stick to back lanes and pop over the A23 on Beech Hill Road. Still no sign of pursuit. I think I lost them at least half a county ago. I'm pretty much set from here. The phone chimes a trill and I pull over to read it, rubbing some warmth back into my torso. Antonio says he's already on his way in, and I should wait in the usual spot. The tightness relaxes a little. The traffic is still quiet enough in places that I can open up and roll some miles under the tyres at a decent speed.

I make it to Blackbushe Airport at a reasonable hour. It's a private airstrip but not in the way that most people imagine. The open field consists of a couple of runways built during the first half of World War Two, only one of which is still operational. A control tower and a couple of pre-fab offices operate as service buildings at one end. It's mainly used for flight instruction and passenger lights, which means those little two- and four-seater propeller planes. I've seen some smaller jets land, but I don't think any live here. No hangers for the mega-rich.

And no helicopters.

It's licensed for night use and is relatively busy, so my comings and goings at all hours don't draw any attention. There are always a few cars standing around, left by pilots who've taken their little planes on a little jaunt to France or Norway. I've met a few of them. They're like model train enthusiasts, with model planes instead. Except the models are big enough to actually fly.

The security cameras are always on the fritz (yeah, sorry about that) and everyone keeps to their own business, more or less. I think half the drugs in the south-east used to come in through here. Then there was this big raid about eight years ago, and now it's mostly legit.

Along with a go-kart track, there's a car auction lot at the opposite end of the airfield to the control tower. That's my first stop. I roll my way discretely down and curl into the customer parking, which is hidden by a higher hedge.

I barely have time to get the helmet off and pick out a few stray hairs when I spy my friend sauntering over. Oh, Antonio, you slender, Italian beast. You can saunter with the best of them. He turns his narrow hips sideways to squeeze through the pedestrian turnstile, then shimmies his suntanned way over. He has a graceful, well-tailored coat over his smart, salesman suit. I haul the bike up onto its main stand, fetch my bag from the box and drop in the helmet.

"Cara Tesorina!"

I smile. "Don't start, you old smoothie," I say, tossing him the keys. He catches them in his wrinkled, olive hands. O! his hands!

There are not many people who can pull off a half smile, while sporting a pencil-thin moustache and that much product in their artificially darkened hair. There are far too many creases in his face, even from that little smirk. When the hell did he get so old?

"I start nowthing, Cucciola! I cannot help where your mind-ah goes every time you see me!"

Mmmm, his eyes still sparkle.

"My mind goes to my purse, mostly to check it's still there."

"As if I would interfere with your purse."

"Hah! Well, that's up for debate. What do you think of the bike?"

Hands on his creaking knees, he bends for better view. "Kawasaki. Relatively new. You have-ah the keys, for a change, eh? Bikes are not the sort of thing we deal with here. It may take-ah me a while."

"I'm in no hurry, my old friend. As long as I get something for it."

"Passerotta!" He starts that Italian gesturing. "You know I made a promise to your dear Mamma that I would always do right by you." He made no such promise. "And I have." Okay, that he has. "But please-ah understand, if you insist on following in her footsteps, mia stella, you may suffer the same-ah fate. You know we were together for but a short time." I wouldn't call five hours short. No seriously. Five. Hours. Hmm. "But we loved a lifetime! I would hate to think of you involving yourself with such-ah terrible people."

"Hey, remember. No-one knows what happened to my mother. And I'm not that involved," I lie. "At least, I'm not obsessed like she was. I just keep my ear to the ground and, look," I indicate the bike, "I'm always careful. Switching cars and transport like you taught me. And I come to no-one but you." Another lie. I have two other people I use for car disposal alone. That's why I had to check my notebook before texting him. "Anyway, it looks like this latest thing isn't going to pan out." Lies, damned lies, but at least no statistics. "I'm just going to have a coffee and head home."

"Please remember, Cucciola. I will not be here-ah forever. Another year, two years, I may have to retire. You should get out while you are still-ah so bella! Ah! You look as young as the day I met you. The spitting image of your dear Mamma! But you too, are getting older. And still no ring."

"Oh, you must stop! I'm not without potential rings." More lies.

"No, but I insist, you must tell me the secret of your youthful looks."

"I stay away from tanning beds, you old prune."

We laugh and chat briefly about this and that. The tightness fades as the spring morning warms me.

I was with Antonio for a couple of months the first time around. Not even half a year. I was trying to learn about cars and such. The old smoothie operated out of a small, lock-up garage in south-east London, tucked under a railway arch. Mostly legit.

I helped him dodge a deportation. In turn, he taught me many things, shall we say. I came back to him over the years, mostly to make use of his services. And, yes, for that, too. It's always good to see him again. Even now, when I'm pretending to be my own daughter, well, grand-daughter, when his aged face makes me feel all weird and uncomfortable.

I leave the bike with my friend. He'll strip it and give me a decent price, directly into my other-other account. No questions asked.

It's a ten minute power-walk to the airport entrance, but I decide I'm not in a hurry any more. It's already late enough for the sun and traffic. I'll miss the early morning BaGua class in the village hall that I use to unwind.

Tucking some dangling hairs from my wig into my bag, I wander down the airfield, past the two- and four-seater prop planes. Their covers make them seem like hooded hunting birds at the side of the runways. I fetch the keys from my hiding spot and open my car, grabbing the bag of spare clothes from the boot. It's an Estate, so the boot has plenty of room, and its not suspicious that I have a sports bag full of sports clothes tucked in there.

I like the fact that people don't look twice at an estate car. This is an older model BMW M3 Sport Touring Estate. Antonio helped me remove all the M-series badges and replace them with 320i badges. Also, I added an in-line electric motor as a turbo, giving another eighty Newton-metres of torque every time I press the pedal. Mostly, I just trundle about in it, carrying clay one way and my pottery the other, to the galleries that sell my work.

Once, I had to put the hammer down and leave some poor bastard in my dust. It was worth it just for that one time. The licence place switcher is based on a couple of stacking CD changers I beefed up a bit.

Do you still own CDs? There's a bunch of mine in the glovebox. I really should get around to digitising my collection but I can't be arsed.

I head over to change in the appropriate porta-cabin. There's never anyone in the women's washroom, and they have showers. Girls still think they should be air hostesses, not pilots. What do they call them these days? Flight Attendants. I prefer to set my own destinations.

There's probably one woman at this airfield of private propeller planes, but I've never met any.

I clean off the blood and dirt and tears. There's a stick tucked into the inside pocket of my jacket, and I remember pushing lungs aside with it. A deep shiver runs through me, but I don't throw up. I don't freak out and scream and throw things. I just tuck it into the Zara bag with the rest of the clothing. Boots, wig, bloody blouse, silk scarf and all. They're for burning on the way home.

Once dry, I slip into slacks, Converse, tank top, and a light puffer. A forgettable combination.

Feeling refreshed, I pop on my sunglasses and wander across to The Bushe café, a prefab that sits near the admin building. I grab some passable coffee and one of their excellent breakfast panini. There's something so damned English about two sausages and a fried egg jammed into expensive Italian bread. God, I love it! Plus it gives me time to go over my notes and try to make sense of what the fuck happened.

# 4

# Village

My nostrils sting with an acrid odour, pulling me from slumber.

But I can't wake up yet.

I'm dreaming about something. Something important.

Very important.

In the dream, I'm moving. Floating between the stars, a pitch-black swirl of chaos with flecks of light. Perspective shifts. It's dark, and I'm driving. Points of rain flash through my headlights, somewhere I remember.

Oh, it's the outer suburbs of Sydney. Australia. I grew up around here for about seven years, when my dad took the promotion, before he moved us back to Stevenage. From the age of five to just after I turned thirteen. Which is why I think in Metric.

I remember the eucalypt smell of gumtrees and the melting heat. I liked the heat.

Australia's a great place to lay low for a bit. Last time I was there I thought of settling but the art scene is too small. Too difficult to blend into invisibly. Plus, I got this interesting tip about a Yakuza gang in London.

I'm still there, in a tiny old Datsun in the dark and rain, except my hands are huge, old and gnarled, like they kept growing and changing while I didn't age.

There's a broad floodplain, fields and woodland on the outskirts of Fairfield, and I'm racing along. Rain. Proper, torrential rain with hail the size of golf-balls, bangs down all around me. I miss this kind of rain. Better a storm over in an hour than a day of dribbling drizzle like in England. I'm racing down a straight, tarmac road. The hail is denting my car except for where I have one huge hand out the window covering the roof like a newspaper over a hurrying head.

The rain makes it even harder to see.

I glance to my left. Moonlight shows me the levee has broken. A low flood of water rushes over flat fields, a confusion of ripples and churning of white. Another car flashes its lights, blinding in the rear-view, the distant blare of a horn, barely audible in the rattle of hail. The driver's trying to warn me.

Something I missed.

Just ahead, the swollen waters of William's Creek challenge their banks, spray jumping. The road rises over the creek via a tiny, humped bridge.

I'll be safe on the bridge.

The car behind won't be so lucky. I'll miss what the driver has to tell me. I want to slow, hear the message, but the wash sweeping towards me over the fields is terrifying. As I'm driving, I become larger and larger, my bulking body pressing against the sides of the cabin, head hunching over, almost bursting out of the car. The engine smokes from the strain. Wait. Smoke.

Ah, shit.

I jerk up into the real world, the dismaying scent of burning pulling me off the slate floor-

Floor? Fuck me.

No, it's okay.

I think.

I'm in my little cottage, lying on the kitchen tiles, chair and table legs like a forest in front of me. I'm lost in the woods again.

Fuck, fuck, fuck. Please don't let me find out the monster killed someone in here. I really don't want to have to fucking move. I just got new curtains.

Burning stings my nostrils.

"Oh! My muffins!" I cry. No, seriously. I actually say that out loud. It's probably the least cool reaction I've ever had to anything. When the fuck did I lose it to the point where I actually give a flying fornication about fucking muffins?

I leap up and turn to see smoke escaping the oven. A brand new Cortina, fan-forced, in that lovely old style with the brass fittings, matching hob and range-hood beside.

Shit, shit, shit. I grab both the trays straight out of the heat. This is why I have heavy, white-lace inner curtains over all the windows, so no one can see me doing things that would burn an ordinary person and leave horrific blisters. Also, the fainting and falling to the floor thing. I live down a dead-end lane to cut back on passing traffic.

The trays go straight onto the granite counter, while my fingers scream at me and I take a little dip into the sun, revelling in a sensation so unimaginable-

A flash of Bright-Eyes in the yard outside the hovel. The image hits me like a physical blow. My hip strikes the table and I realise I've staggered a couple of steps. I catch myself, stay upright, and don't pass out.

The phone? Something about when he was speaking on the phone.

I take a couple of breaths. Well. I don't know who Bright-Eyes was talking to or what he said. That was a couple of nights ago. However, something in me gleaned more details about that encounter than my human brain registered. I might have put it together from lip reading, the faintest noise, body-language.

Damn, but I need a drink. There's no cup of water laid out. This fit must have taken me by surprise. Well, obviously. Muffins destroyed. I grab a mug, fill it from the tap, chugging it all down. It flows into me and that inner awareness is calming.

I am here. I work. I function.

When I swallow liquid it goes down.

It's strange to have doubts about even something so simple as that. I have no idea why my body functions the way it does, I doubt the very nature of the world, but then I stub my fucking toe and hey! Yep. Sideboards are real.

My notebook flops on the table, pencil beside. My insight about Bright-Eyes will be in there, somewhere, buried in the mess. It's full of scribblings that don't even remotely resemble my handwriting, pages of symbols and marks that don't belong to any human language. Or the language of any recognisable living organism. Possibly they indicate which portions of an energy field should be simultaneously issuing a number of musical notes. Later, I'll try playing it upstairs on my piano.

I pick up the little black book and scribble a bracket on the corner, flip back to the last interval marking. About five pages worth.

While waiting for the muffins, I had a fit and started up with that automatic-writing bullshit. Passed out. Ended up on the floor.

Fuck. My. Life.

At least there isn't a dead body to deal with. Probably. I half-sit at the kitchen table to go over the notes in detail, then remember the muffins, the fucking coffee morning, and all the shit in my other life.

*Rat-a-tat-tat* comes the polite little knock on the quaint door of my picturesque cottage.

Yeah. This is the other half of my existence. The cover. The charade. Elstead. I live in a lovely country village in the Garden of England. The Surrey Hills are officially an Area of Outstanding Natural Beauty (AONB), around two hours outside London, or fifty minutes to Godalming on the express from Waterloo, then a fifteen minute drive. Well, twenty minutes the way you drive.

A lot of rolling fields, ordered woodlands, and way too many opportunities to use the word 'quaint' when describing buildings.

I kinda like it.

When I was studying art, I took an extension in pottery. Years later I came back to it, mostly as a way to launder my other income, but I really enjoy making things in clay. It sits on that fascinating border between craft and art. There's only so many things you can make the clay do. Structurally. You have to build it. I like to keep an edge of refinement to the lines of my pots, vases and occasional sculptures. The local beauty, natural and man-made, is constantly inspiring: colours, textures, ideas. I get the best ideas for glazes when I'm out on my walks.

Oh, wait.

Muffins.

Knocking.

Reality.

"Door's open!" I call, stepping back to the trays and waving a tea-towel with a pineapple print.

"Hello, hello!" comes the chirpy chirp announcing the arrival of Susan's skinny arse. She's not reliable or even remotely trustworthy, but she's a good way to pass the time, hear the gossip, spread rumours and alibis. It's almost normal.

She bounces in wearing her best leggings, trainers, and purple, wind-resistant jacket. I mentioned I like purple, and Sue now wears it every time she comes to see me, all perky and smiling in spite of that nose of hers. It's what I like about her the most. Not the nose. Seriously, no-one could ever like that nose. Neither of her husbands did. The perkiness in spite of it inspires me. It's so very English, and smacks faintly of brittle desperation.

"Oh, my god! You're burning something!"

"Fucking muffins," I tell her. "Wandered into the other room to jot down some design ideas." I wave the notebook. "Lost track of time."

"This is why you need a smoke detector!" Her sing-song theme rings (wrings) a sneer from me.

"I fucking hate smoke alarms!" I sing back at her.

Sue shakes her head. "You can't turn up to the bake sale empty handed after you promised Margaret cakes. That old bitch will never forgive you!"

"I could just make a donation. What the fuck are we raising money for this time, anyway?"

"It's the Hospital Auxiliary."

"The what now?"

"Hospital Auxiliary. They help out at the hospital. Volunteers."

"If they're volunteers, why the fuck do they need money?"

"No, don't be silly. The Hospital Auxiliary is raising money for the hospital. Margaret's in that as well as the WI. They're buying some new, um, kidney machine, or something. There's one of those big thermometer things on the wall in the hospital cafeteria, showing how much they've raised and how far they have to go. The school did a Mufti day for it and everything. It's well over half-way, now. We can give them a real boost. Oh, god, it's worse than I thought. They're all black."

Sue's nose curls up in disgust at the sight of my maladroit muffins emerging from the smoke haze. And with that schnoz of hers, it's a whole other level of revulsion.

"Well, that's it," she says. "You'll have to commit suicide."

"Nah, fuck that. I can fix this."

"Oh, no way! They're burnt to a crisp!"

"Prepare to be amazed by some baking magic."

I grab things from drawers and cupboards, muttering curses under my breath. Milk and icing sugar, mixing bowls, some chocolate powder, coconut.

"You're going to help," I tell the fascinated Sue.

"Oh, goody!" she replies, and literally bounces with happiness. See this? This is why the monster tears people's heads off.

I ended up in Elstead because there was a house nearby, in a back-lane rented from some farm. They call them 'Training Houses', where they gang rape the girls five times a day and get them addicted to heroin. Once the poor bitches are broken, they ship them off to whichever city gang will pay the most. I based myself at The Mill-on-the-Wey while I was investigating, and fell in love with the twee-ness of it all. So I moved in.

"You know how to make a chocolate glaze?" I ask Sue.

"Absolutely! I do a mean chocolate glaze."

"Fan-fucking-tastic. You get on with that; I'm going to hack what I can out of these muffins."

"Won't it be all horribly dry?"

"Yep," I tell her, as I pick up the bread knife and start slicing. "That's why I'm going to make a syrup coating and soak them in that, maybe even put some of Old Christine's blueberry jam in the middle. Then we coat them in chocolate, roll them in the coconut and call them fruit lamingtons."

"Fruit what?"

"Lamingtons. It's an Australian thing. Usually, you make them with sponge, not muffin, but what the fuck would this lot know? I'll just tell them it's an old family recipe."

We set to work and I manage to rescue a decent chunk from the middle of most of the muffins. I made two trays of the damn things. I wanted some for myself. Even with two muffin rescues per lamington, there's still a decent amount.

Somewhere in the middle of it all I casually pick up the one piece of seriously incriminating evidence I seem to have left lying around, flick the notebook shut, and pop it into a random drawer. I check the last page before I drop it, and almost forget to slide the drawer closed.

He said "Ma'am."

Bright-Eyes. On the phone. I can see it clear as day. His mouth forming and articulating the word 'Ma'am'. How the fuck is there a lady involved in all of this? Am I still at the pimp stage? Aren't we past that? I track pimps until I find one professional enough to take requests from specialist buyers. Now there's a woman buyer? I've never, in all my years-

"Your notes must be really interesting."

Oh, wait. Baking. Sue. Fuck.

"Ah, yeah. But let's get these lamingtons out of the way."

We carefully pack the serving dish into a little wicker basket, lined with a red and white chequered cloth. I drape the tea towel over the top, then Sue and I set off, arm in arm - no, seriously - and wander down the lane to the British Legion hall where today's bake sale resides.

It's a beautiful spring day. I'm out for a walk in a picturesque country village with someone I might hesitate to kill. All the houses in my lane have hanging baskets of flowers providing a riot of colours. Lovely.

You can tell that something shitty is about to happen, can't you?

The women have the bake sale well on the way to set up, with all the usual barely-concealed tensions and rivalries subjugated into petty bickering over table placements and who should be making the coffees. Even old Effie manages to rock about on her damaged, metre-wide hips without too much complaining, though she does ask awkward questions about why I don't have a husband yet.

As an astute observer of humanity, from a somewhat outside perspective, I find it all fascinating, highly amusing, and depressing.

These are the people who vote for the political Right. Many of them drove their cakes half a mile to the bake sale in huge, pollution-belching, four-wheel drive monsters. Caring, charitable, generous, racist, homophobic, clueless bitches.

This is how the world will end. People like this squabbling over tables while handing over power to a bunch of rich, privileged, climate-change-denying bastards, determined to line their own pockets. Because that's all it's in their nature to do. And I'm too addicted to my own petty revenges to step up.

I could change the world but I don't.

My lamingtons sell like hotcakes. Which is ironic, because the hotcakes don't sell very well at all. Bitch Margaret is suitably impressed and full of praise for everyone. She'll let us know how much has been raised once she adds it all up and secretly slips herself an easy twenty.

Groceries are so expensive, these days.

I help with the packing away, chatting with the ladies about my latest pottery commission-slash-alibi. I have to travel up to London to interview some student helpers, speak with the faculty, and book kiln time at the University for a larger project.

Actually, I'm going to make a trip back to the rotting cottage, now things have settled down. It's been a couple of days since my car chase and body dump. Nothing in the papers or police reports, so the cottage might still be in use. They think they've scared me off. Or the building's an empty shell and I'll have to start over.

The University story is just my usual cover. But I will get to see my Puppy.

Sue and I leave the hall, bitching about everyone behind their backs and chatting about the latest episode of *Yorkshire Vet*. Yeah, no. I don't find the show that interesting, but I have to watch it, so I have something to gossip about. That's the sum total of my modern TV viewing, now that *Buffy*'s finished. Oh, there was that *True Detective*. I liked that, for obvious reasons. The second season wasn't nearly as good, so I stopped there.

I don't have much in the way of spare time. It's the same with all people who produce, who make stuff, who have something to do with their lives. We don't have as much time to consume. And, my god, there is so much to consume! It's one of the things I enjoy about my condition. Even being busy, I have more time for reading, watching, seeing, travelling. While doing my pottery, I listen to books on tape. What do they call them these days? Audiobooks. I'll still never get around to it all.

A single fluffy, white cloud drifts lazily across the afternoon sky.

My stomach growls. Hungry. My bowels seem to work, that whole system. I tried going a week without food once, just to see. I made it barely three days before I was faint and trembling with the sun. So, I still function like a regular person. My hair grows, only much, much slower. So do my fingernails. It cuts back on trips to the beauty parlour.

Sue wants to make us some pasta, then she'll head home and leave me to my preparation work. We might have some wine. I still function, so I can get drunk eventually. It takes much, much, much longer. Pretending I'm drunk or drugged is how I get alone time with most of my prey.

We reach the top of my lane, which is narrow and has a double bend, winding behind what was the farmhouse but is now a row of town-houses. The land was subdivided and built-up after this section of village was hit by some misguided bombs during World War Two. Part of the 50's redevelopment, that second layer of destruction caused by the Second World War, a stain on every part of England that might never be erased. The other side of the main road, here, is not very picturesque. My little lane of converted, seventeenth-century stables and farm-buildings survived.

England prevails.

We curl around and I'm crapping on about the difference between electric cars and internal combustion engines. I've no idea how we got onto the topic. I visited a KIA showroom in London on my last trip. The GT version of the EV6 is bonkers. Zero to a hundred kph in three-and-half seconds. In a fucking SUV. And it's not bad around the corners. If Antonio can get the badging off that, it would be a fantastic, stealth getaway car for me. Also great for transporting clay and pottery. But there's the whole GPS thing.

"No, but seriously, I was really fucking impressed!" I tell Sue, clutching my wicker basket in folded arms. "And that little MG Cyberster thingy goes like shit off a shovel!" I visited MG, too. "Not very practical for me, but that KIA? Decent sized SUV. Holy crap is that awesome! And I won't have to give that little Tesla troll any of my hard-earned money. Fuck those petrol cars. Just fuck 'em all!"

Sue is in stitches, laughing and snorting uncontrollably. I've no idea what's so funny but I'm laughing too.

"Oh god, you know I love you, my sweet," she says, "but you have to stop swearing so much!"

"Hey, I was polite as fuck in during the bake sale."

"Oh, positively restrained you were. Did you injure yourself?"

"Very nearly! Oh, now what the fuck is up with these thundercunts?"

A huge four-by-four blocks the entire lane, all black and shiny. "Typical country wankers," I declare. "How the fuck is anyone supposed to get past?" Wait. My hands go cold. I swallow a dry lump. Big. Black. Oh, shit. It's a Range Rover.

# 5

# Studio

I cover the fact that I'm freaking out inside by yelling, "Hey, you're blocking the whole damned lane with that thing, you know?"

Sue is spluttering with hysteria and trying to restrain me. Meanwhile, my mind is racing, thinking of exit strategies.

I can clear that fence into Norman's yard, sprint for the village green. I might be able to sneak my way over the fields to Godalming, where I hid my car for this evening's excursion. Is it even there any-more? Did they find that too?

Perhaps I can use Sue as a hostage.

A man wanders around the side, unabashed at my yelling, carrying himself with some authority.

Fucking cop. I'll bet my life.

I try to hide my sigh of relief. The kind of nasties I hunt don't drag the police into their business. Don't get me wrong, they pay off the right people, but that doesn't give them access to any official resources. In any case, the sort I'm ultimately interested in are not the ones who traffic people and drugs.

"Hello, there," he says and flashes quite a charming smile along with his ID. The smart-casual-but-with-a-tie look he's sporting is a step up from the usual polyester suit. Good teeth.

Great hair.

An interesting face. Not too clean and GQ. "I'm Detective Sergeant Daniel Ripplewater, I'm looking for-"

"Yeah, yeah," I cut in. "You're looking for me. Because my fucking mother has gone and done something batshit crazy, and, for some insane reason, you think you might get some information out of me this time! Instead of the nothing-at-all you got from me all the other half a dozen times!" I turn to my accomplice. "You should probably head home, Suzie. It's going to take ages to go through this bullshit."

In the reflection of the bay window of my cottage, I spy Bright-Eyes lurking on the other side of the car.

I allow myself the panic of recognition underneath my rant, getting it out of the way, so I can keep my cool when he confronts me to provoke a reaction.

The sexy detective didn't introduce him, and this isn't the kind of car a detective could afford, so I'm guessing neither of them are here in any official capacity. Still, I should be able to get this over with quickly. I've got to stay cool, keep my breathing soft, face relaxed, posture confident, make sure the freaking-out bits of me stay buried deep.

"Miss," Dan the Cute says, "this is a very serious matter. You really need to stop with the swearing."

"Oh, bullshit! You can't just keep harassing me every fucking time my stupid fucking mother-"

"Miss! Now, that's enough. I can charge you with-"

"Charge me? I should be able to charge you! Isn't there, like, some statue thingy where you can't keep harassing someone for the same old bullshit? Or do you think she's killed someone new?"

"In the UK there is a Limitations Act, not a sta-tute, and there's no limitations on murder. Now, get yourself under control."

Professional and commanding. I kinda like that. I take a deep breath, let out a sigh, drop the attitude and go into apologetic mode. Remember?

"You know, you're right. I apologise. I'm sorry. Knowing my mother, this probably is a serious matter, and you're just doing your job. Sorry. It gets very frustrating being put through the wringer every couple of years. No-one likes to be reminded they got abandoned as a child."

He seems momentarily stumped by my magnanimous attitude and hint of a tragic backstory. Sue is standing patiently to one side, half enjoying the show and half not wanting to get dragged into a murder inquiry.

I turn to my bake-sale buddy, squeezing her arm and gently nudging her away. "It's okay, Sue. We'll do lunch another time and I'll tell you all about it, yeah?"

"Well, I... Okay. Sure." Susan slides away, glancing back a couple of times, mostly to get a look at the cute cop, showing off exactly the wrong angle for that nose of hers.

"So, is it Detective? Sergeant Ripplewater?" How fantastic a name is Ripplewater? I glance at my car, gaze lingering for a moment, then back to him. "What do I call you?"

"Detective's fine, miss. I just wanted to ask a few questions." He relaxes into his role. "Is this your car?"

Oh, yeah. He's going to be so easy to manipulate. I mean, if you seriously think I don't know about the Magistrates Court Act of 1980 as it applies to murder then you haven't been following along properly. They love to correct statue to statute. Makes them feel all manly and superior. I'll walk him through, get what information I can, and see if I can set him off on the wrong track.

Damn, but he's cute, though! I wonder if I can get his pants off within the hour? I probably could, but then there's Bright-Eyes and I'm not into threesomes.

"Yeah. I got it about a five years ago. I wanted to get one of those big Hyundai thingies, y'know, like Dr Foster drives, do you watch *Dr Foster*?"

"Ah, no. I don't have much time for television in my job."

"Ha! Me neither. But, yeah, too expensive. This was a bargain. A friend of mine at a car auction lot replaced the ruined gearbox." Or, at least, that's what it says on the invoice. "Now it runs a treat."

"Alloy wheels, leather interior. Nice. Does it have GPS?"

Oh, he's smart. I like that. He wants to be able to check where I've been. "Well, no. It's an earlier model, before the GPS was standard. I have great GPS on my phone, though. I made do with a Focus for a while, but there's just not enough room in the back of one of those, especially since I'm getting larger commissions."

"Commissions? For what, exactly?"

"Oh, I'm a ceramicist."

"A... Sorry, a what?"

"Ceramicist. I work with ceramics. Y'know, pottery and stuff." I gesture to the door. Yes. That's it. Follow my hand. "The house is basically my studio-slash-workshop. Oh, you probably shouldn't come in. I haven't had a chance to clean up the mess I made before the bake-sale."

"This is a serious matter, miss," he says, eyes all stern. "I think it would be best if we went inside."

That's right. You're the boss. Police get this training where they're taught to take control of a situation and stay in charge. For most of them that means making people do the opposite of what they want. You have to be subtle about it, but if you really want a police officer to let you go, try to convince them they should keep you around. I want to get this off the street, into my kitchen, where I have weapons to hand.

"No, seriously. I burned the muffins. It's like a bomb hit it. I really don't know anything. I haven't seen her in years."

"Please miss, it'll just take a few moments." Ripplewater steps back and gestures towards the door.

Huh. Good use of a non-committal time frame. He's sticking to the standard police lines so far. No hint of personality to go along with that interesting choice of shirt. Just professionalism. I'm going to have to be careful with this one.

"Well, don't say I didn't warn you," I reply, shaking my head in exasperation. I walk around the Range Rover and Bright-Eyes looms suddenly. I give him a blank, annoyed stare. The trick is to stay soft, not put on hard faces. "Is he with you?" I ask Detective Dan.

"Oh, sorry, yes. This is my, er, colleague, Mr Smith. He's from a different division. We're consulting."

"Oh, okay. Hi." I nod an awkward greeting and immediately dismiss him, making sure to never look at him again, so he knows he's not important to me. Instead, I stare at the huge car as I'm walking past, then glance down the lane, a quick look back to the car while I fish for my keys.

"You should probably wait in the car," Dan the man in charge says to his 'colleague', "in case someone needs to get past."

Bright-Eyes grunts in annoyance. I'm not going to call him Smith because it's not good to name them and, in any case, that's definitely not his name. "Just find out what she knows," he says.

Ah. So. He's the one who's really in charge.

This doesn't make sense. Bright-Eyes is not a cop. That Brioni sports jacket over the Armani turtleneck, some designer brand khakis with hand-made shoes, that's Dan's salary for a month. Two, maybe. And who wears a fucking turtleneck? But Dan is a real detective and, in spite of my little manipulations, his intelligence rings true.

Is he even corrupt at all? If not, what's he doing hanging out with some ex-army thug associated with the kind of people I'm tracking?

Well, let's get this show off the road and find out.

"Why do you have a cartoon picture of a woman with a pineapple on your keychain?" Dan asks, as we enter my kitchen. It's as good a conversation starter as any, though it does give away how closely he's observing me.

"Huh? Oh, very observant of you. Takasugi Naoko. Japanese motorcycle racer."

"Right. That's a thing, is it?"

I shoulder the door closed and wander over to the kitchen table.

"Not really, no. I was in Japan a few years ago, researching original raku-firing methods and met her in a supermarket." Actually, I was doing clean-up on some of Puppy's friends. You'll meet Puppy in a minute. She's nice. "Trying to decide between instant noodle dinners, standing there with a one in each hand. This little Japanese girl with frizzy, dyed-blonde hair is waiting for me to get out of the way. They call her The Pineapple, because her hair looks like one. I asked her, like you do when you can't speak the language properly with my hands, which one should I pick." I drop the basket onto the table, and do the gesture for him "This or this? She shook her head and pointed to another one entirely. Long story short, I ended up in her crew pit a week later, chatting with one of the umbrella girls whose father ran a pottery works on the other side of the mountain. Scored a key chain. Oh, and that tea-towel."

Dan has a polite but unreadable expression on his face as he blinks, looking around. It's a fascinating little tale. I have a whole bunch of fun bits I can add to flesh it out. Who wouldn't want to hear about a female Japanese motorcycle racer? But he's a man. Women talking is all aimless chatter to him.

Ready for the sob-story? I've got this whole character background worked out. All corroborated with scant online evidence. I seldom get the chance to share.

"Wow, you weren't kidding about the mess," Detective Daniel Ripplewater comments, eyebrows raised. "That's almost impressive."

"Oh, you're hilarious." Hah! The first crack in his armour, the moment he's away from Bright-Eyes. That's revealing in itself. "Sue and I spent the morning rescuing my disaster. I didn't have time to tidy. Here, let me, um..." I grab a few utensils and bowls and shuffle them into the sink, all embarrassed. "I'm usually quite clean."

"No, that's fine, miss. Perhaps we could go through and sit?"

"Oh, no, no. That's the studio. The sitting room is upstairs, through that door there."

"Do you mind if I take a quick look at the studio?"

He is so easy to manoeuvre. Now, I'll be able to ramble on about my pottery, already set up as a favourite subject by the Naoko story, and emphasise my complete lack of connection to any crimes my 'mother' may have committed.

"Er, yeah. I guess. It's just my ceramics stuff."

There's something about him that still bugs me. I can't get a read, get a character, get anything other than simple professionalism. An occasional, vaguely-not-serious statement, but that could just be learned interrogation technique.

The less I get to know him, the better. He seems to be following the right path of realising I had nothing to do with anything.

I lift the latch and walk through. I have latches on all the internal doors, rather than doorknobs.

So cottage. Much rustic.

The studio is tidy, exposed stone-masonry but with a lot of open shelving where moulds sit and work lasts set. The display section at the front has some good pieces. I'm in the middle of a dinnerware run at the moment, so there's a bit on display.

"Okay." Dan looks impressed, like he was expecting some spinster with a hobby. "That's quite the fire-thingy, kiln, you have."

"Oh, yes. One of my better purchases. Programmed slow cooling, eighteen-segment ramp-hold." He nods blankly. "It's a little small, but fine for things like the dinnerware I'm doing, up to the mid-size vases. I mostly use this for the main firing before I apply the raku-work and over-glazes."

"Over-glazes?"

I think he's just trying to get me relaxed, so I start rambling.

"Well, I use a marbling of the clays and different over-slips to influence the variegations in the raku-firing. Gives them these strong colour bands, like this one." I show him my display vase.

"Oh. Interesting shape," he says, leaning in and absently ruffling his hair. Did I mention? Nice hair.

My display piece is an oval, wide at the bottom, tapering slightly before rising straight to the inward-curving top.

"Thank you. It's a development of a Japanese design, hand-shaped rather than thrown on a wheel, so I can use different types of clay all the way through. Then, once the base colouring is on, I polish it back, and apply a semi-transparent over-glaze while the pot is still cooling. Like a filter on a camera lens. The colour-wash helps emphasise the striations and bring out specific tones. I mean, filters are mostly done in Photoshop, these days, but they used to put them on the lenses."

"You polish it while it's cooling? That sounds dangerous."

There's that sharpness, again.

"It's more difficult than dangerous. I use a rotary sander, buff it with polishing powder. You have to be very delicate."

I actually use my fingers and emery paper to do it by touch, but that would scorch a normal person down to the bone.

"I have to put the piece back in the kiln a few times," I continue. "I do burn myself but the results are amazing! Um, even if I do say so myself."

"Oh, no, no. That is beautiful. Really nice. How much does something like that go for?"

He thinks he's sneaking information out of me, like my income, daily activities and so on. I tell him what I want him to hear.

"Oh, a mid-size vase? Depends greatly on how well the process works. Raku is notoriously unpredictable. And you break a lot with the differential temperature thing. Mix of clays. A good one will go for a couple of grand. Something of that quality? Maybe five."

"Five thousand pounds?"

"Oh, yes, but it takes about a month, plus all the conceptual work and preparation. I have to buy the clay, and the quality stuff is expensive. Plus my electricity bill for the kiln is ridiculous. I don't know if you've noticed electricity prices, recently, but damn! That's why I had all those solar panels on the roof. I'll do, maybe, five vases in a year, a couple at top quality that I place in London. The dinnerware set will go for about five hundred to a thousand. Again, depending on how well the pieces turn out. But with these,

I can collect them into good sets for the London galleries, and also good, but not quite as balanced or strong for the local gallery in Godalming. My larger commissions, like the one I have coming up for the Swedish Ambassador, I'll charge up to twenty grand. I only get one of those a year, if that. Maybe two. But they're costly to produce. I have to hire an external kiln, helpers, and so on."

Come to think of it, that is close enough to being the truth these days. I'm doing okay, money-wise, even without robbing headless corpses. The big amounts come from taking down a ring on my way through, and raiding their safe. That can nab me a hefty chunk of change, hence the regular 'larger' pieces that use other kilns, so no-one ever sees them and I can deposit a healthy amount into my account.

"I do the dinnerware in between inspirations and commissions."

"Is there a big demand for your work?"

"Well, my grandmother," who is actually my mother. You've worked this out by now, haven't you? "once said to me, she said," oh, fuck! What name am I using at the moment? I've drawn a blank! "Child, she said, you should just make what you want, and if other people like them, that's a bonus."

"And do people like them?"

"Well, I own my own mortgage."

He glances around the cottage and nods, peering closer at a bowl. Did the whole Swedish Ambassador bit register? Friends in high places, Mr Interesting Shirt. Back off. "What's this writing? Is that Sanskrit or something?"

"Sanskrit? No. It's nothing like it. Here, I'll show you."

I beckon him back out to the kitchen, where I take a risk, open the drawer and pull out my little black book, flicking quickly to a page that's all that 'other' writing. He wanders in, looking genuinely interested.

"I do this sort of automatic-writing thing where I scribble a load of gibberish and come up with these weird characters, then try and string them into a sort of syntax. It's like I'm channelling an alien scribe or something. And I use that for the scroll-work around the pots. Well, those of them that need something that fussy."

He glances, mystified, at the book but doesn't take it from me. He's not interested in the things I'm showing him. He wants to know what I'm not showing him.

"Are you worried what will happen when the aliens turn up and try to read your pots?" he asks.

"Hah! They'll probably arrest me for inadvertently saying nasty things about their mothers." Come on! How many times to I have to say 'mother'? "But, yeah, that's what I was doing when I lost track of time and burnt the muffins."

"Speaking of mothers," he says.

"Oh, smooth transition."

"Thank you." He's a bit cheeky, this one. Not exactly charming, or a comedian, but a playful edge that he can't seem to bury completely. "But it really would be in your mother's best interest-"

"What a wonderfully formal way of putting that. Look. I don't keep in touch with her. I never hear from her. I don't get anything from her except my good looks. Apparently, there's a family resemblance. Especially around the eyes." I tilt my chin up and flutter my eyelashes. "What do you think?"

"We don't-" He has to glance away. Ooo. He's having trouble staying professional. "There doesn't seem to be a picture on file. A recent picture. All we have is her last school photo and that's decades old. We were hoping for something more recent, if you have one."

"Oh, for fuck's sake. I don't have a photo of the crazy woman who ruined my life!"

"Hey, now." He leans against the kitchen table, all friendly-like. "She's mixed up with some very powerful people."

"Great. I hope they do horrible things to her and then kill her."

Dan is taken aback. "That a very harsh attitude to have towards your mother."

"Well, it's not like I ever met the woman." Seriously, now I'm picking up the habit of saying 'well' at the beginning of every fucking sentence. "Not really. All I know about her is she dumped me with my grandmother in Australia when I was, like, five years old, and every couple of years someone in a suit turns up to make me feel uncomfortable for an hour before buggering off. Today, that's your job."

"Well." See? It's a disease! I've infected him, now! "I also find it difficult to imagine that she hasn't tried to keep in touch with you in some way."

"Y'know, Detective, you could be right. Maybe I should check my Facebook for unusual friend requests." I swipe at the air in front of me, scrolling through an imaginary Facebook feed. "No, no, no, nothing. Oh, look! Cheap sunglasses! No, no, nope." I stop swiping. "Nothing there. Or on my Mastodon. Or my Instagram. I'm not even on Pinterest, but the last guy checked that, too." Dan seems despondent. "I'm sure whichever pimp she's dismembered this time has a family that deserves closure, or whatever, but there's really nothing I can do."

"It's not like that." Oh, it is like that Detective Dan, you're not fooling anyone. "This is a missing person's case, but considering your mother's involvement, Mr Smith decided to include me on his team. I work Buckinghamshire CID out of-"

"Buckinghamshire? That's bloody miles away! Wait, do they even have pimps in Buckinghamshire?"

"Sorry, miss, but why do you think it's a pimp?"

"Well, the last three or four were pimps, and Lord What's-his-face from ten years ago is in the middle of this posh-people's child-molestation inquiry. My mother seems to have a very particular type."

"The person who's missing is a private security guard. Your mother was trying to break into a property. He went to investigate, now he's missing. She might have stolen his car."

"Yeah? If that was my mother, you'd be better off investigating the property, believe me. And why do you think that's my mother anyway? Stray hair caught in the hedgerow? She prick herself on some barbed wire?"

"No, we found her fingerprints at the scene."

"Fingerprints?" Bullshit! I do not leave fingerprints! You saw me wipe that fucking car down, right? "How terribly old fashioned."

"Still effective. We don't have, er… Well. She seems to have bugged out in a bit of hurry by a country lane, left her prints on the metal gate as she was rushing through."

Oh! The gate! The fucking gate! When I jumped out to, "That was careless of her," open the gate with Bright-Eyes charging down on me and FUCK!

"Well. No matter how good someone is, their luck always runs out."

Fucking gate! "I'm sure that's case. And I'll tell you what." Motherfucking stupid fucking fuck! "If I ever see the woman who has had no contact with me whatsoever in the past thirty years, you'll be the first person I tell."

"Sorry, miss, but we have to ask these questions in a case that involves, things. A case like this."

Now he's starting to wonder what kind of case this really is.

Hang on.

GATE. GATE. GATE. GATE. FUCK!

Sorry.

I'm getting the impression that poor Detective Dan has been duped. He doesn't know what his friend Bright-Eyes gets up to at night.

Also, they don't have my DNA on file, no recent pictures, and they haven't found the burnt-out car in Reading or, if they have, they haven't connected it to Headless. And they haven't found Headless. Looks like that old man with his dog gets to live after all. 'Bugged out' is a military term, so that might be where he knows Bright-Eyes. Their interaction outside suggests a different unit, or different rank.

All interesting stuff.

And yes, I did memorise the licence plate on the Range Rover this time. I traced it onto my palm with a fingernail to make sure it sticks.

"Well, Detective, I'm not sure how many other ways there are for me to say the same thing."

Dan the Dupe wears a thoughtful expression but he's still present enough to register my dismissal and not like it. Annoyance flashes in his eyes as one hand covers his pocket. What's he doing? Feeling his notebook? What's the matter? Nothing to write down? Oh, it's his phone! He's recording this on his phone. How sweet.

If he's read the reports on me, he should already know he's not getting any information. Then his eyes rest on the burnt muffin bits, and maybe he remembers the bit about the Swedish Ambassador. He deflates. Yes, that's right. Domestically incompetent niche artist living in a quaint country cottage with powerful friends. More trouble than I'm worth, me.

Now fuck off.

"I'm sorry to have bothered you, miss. This is clearly a waste of time. A couple of my other colleagues are following up some alternative leads. I'll, er, I'll let you know if we find anything."

"Yes. Well. Thank you. For, er, for being so," I give him a little flicker of embarrassed eye contact, "nice about it. It's a horrible job, I know."

He seems a little flustered. "Well, er, I'll be in touch."

"Please do." The which means I'm never going to hear from him, again. And delightfully droll, deluded Detective Dan shuffles awkwardly out the door, nodding politely as he leaves.

Shit. I probably could have gotten his pants off.

I barely got to reveal any of my sob-story. Disappointing!

It's difficult to get a read on him. He was professional. That's about it. The slightly interesting clothes, that little spark of humour, the confident way he carried himself, all point to something more. The hair. It made an impression but I'm not sure what's underneath.

Well, no time to- SEE! I'm going to stop saying 'well' every other fucking sentence! I'm also still annoyed about that fucking gate, but I get down to the business of cleaning my kitchen, a nice, domestic shape barely visible through the heavy, white lace as the big, black Range Rover does an awkward turn in Mrs Chester's empty car-space.

It's at least a six-point turn.

I'm sure Bright-Eyes is staring at me.

Watching the entertainment with a certain smug glee, I'm sure neither of them will want to come back down this twisty little lane again in a hurry. I'm disappointed about that in the case of Dan, but I get the feeling I'll be seeing Bright-Eyes shortly.

I look down and it's just the clean-up. Crumbs everywhere and twice as many bowls because we had to do more icing. That's always the case with me. It's always the clean-up.

Because of my daemon, I only ever get a glimpse of what it is I do. Everything else is lost in the pleasure. So much bliss that this miss passes out. I wake in the mess and have to deal with that.

I never get to really experience the joys of baking, the utter satisfaction of doing the act, the flavours and textures before the end product settles in. Like a kitchen-hand in the world's top restaurant, I can never truly savour the exquisite nature of the dishes. I'm just standing here with the mess in the bowls.

After I've collected the crockery and set it soaking in the sink, I damp down a scouring pad and start scrubbing the beautiful surfaces. I don't stop until I can see a distortion of my face in them.

# 6

# Countryside

The three-twenty-six to Waterloo smells like the toilet backed up. Water is leaking into the carriage. The whole fucking train smells like that. First class has its advantages, but a niche artist regularly booking the most expensive seats is not an innocent look. I suffer the slight odour of decay.

The tannoy at the terminal is broken, distorting all the announcements. Cars snarl and grind their way down Waterloo Road, but the station entrance contains one bright point.

Meet Puppy. She's what people think a student should look like: hair shaved on one side, the rest dyed blue, tall for an Asian girl, punk leather jacket from Camden, tartan skirt, black leggings tucked into her Doc Martins. Her hipster sunglasses are colour coordinated with her nose-stud. We hug like we haven't seen each other in ages.

"It's been a minute," she says, her home-counties accent rich with happiness.

"A couple of ticks," I reply. "It's good to see you, too, babe."

"Hah! You only ever call me when you want something."

"Given how often you call me in the wee hours of the fucking morning, I think we're about even."

She laughs and we head down to one of those side streets behind the Old Vic where you can cheekily park for five minutes without a resident's permit, especially if you have an electric car. And none of those all-pervading security cameras.

"Wee is Scotland? Means small?"

"Scottish."

"Scottish, yeah. Speak in Scotland, Scottish." She blinks and darkness creeps into her face for a moment. "You... You don't mind? 'Small hours' is the middle of night, yeah? I won't-"

Her English slips when the anxiety overtakes her.

"No, no. It's fine, babe." I give her back a rub. "You call me whenever. Don't even think about it. How's the coursework going?"

She needs a moment to come back. I give her as long as she likes.

Puppy was born in Shandong province, in China, just north of Qingdao Port. Her parents wanted a fancy new TV so they sold her to a Yakuza comfort house when she was nine. Apparently girl-children are discouraged and can be a burden.

There's a thing in China that, if you fuck a virgin, it will cure you of, well, whatever disease you want to use to justify fucking a nine-year-old. Mostly old age. A couple of mamasans held her down, while rich old men paid a premium to cover her body, their old man tits bigger than hers swaying above her face, and she pretended this hadn't happened two or three times a night before she was eleven. Sex with a thousand different men, and still a virgin.

It's a miracle.

Except Puppy (that's officially her name now) stopped bothering to pretend after a couple of years. The rich old men complained she no longer felt 'tight enough'. The comfort house sold her to the local bossman. Her taller stature, even at that age, made her a decent enough property.

The Yakuza boss shipped her to Japan as a plaything for some of his underlings. Her yoni was too loose for them. They sodomized her instead.

When she turned sixteen, after her final growth-spurt, one young boss took a shine to her momo jiri, peach arse, and brought her to London as his companion while he sorted out some problems with their money laundering.

She was a proper companion now, learned in calligraphy, tea ceremony, bondage, and staring at the world with hollow eyes from the deepest pit of despair. She read widely, though mostly in secret. Chemistry was her favourite subject.

The Yakuza don't have a large physical presence in the UK, but London is a massive cleaning house for a lot of organized crime money. Bratva, Golden Circle, you name it. It's the main reason the UK wanted to keep the pound after they joined the European Union. The currency exchanges keep Interpol from being able to trace the cash-flow too easily. Or did you think it had something to do with national pride?

I was on the hunt a couple of years ago, watching their operation on a tip-off. The Yakuza go through girls like butter. She ran away. They chased her. I chased everyone. It didn't end well for them. She'd stolen a lot of cash. Brand new Great British Pounds. I helped her use it to set up a different identity: passport, birth certificate, National Insurance number, drivers licence. I have a contact, Bas, who's good with computers.

We also set up a false trail into France. A doctor friend of mine in Germany helped us steal the corpse of a Chinese prostitute from a morgue in Mannheim. We burned the corpse in a training house used by some pimps out of Dijon, circulated a little of the money around currency exchange establishments frequented by the Dijon Gitans. French traveller gangs.

The Yakuza reached out to the French Corsican Mafia and wiped out that particular gang. They found some of their money, but the bulk of it is still missing. I mean, I know where it is, but to them it's missing. The Yakuza suspect the Corsican Mafia, who suspect another traveller gang.

Chaos is fun.

You might have read about a spate of gang-related murders in eastern France a while back.

Puppy's English was already pretty good, albeit with a limited but colourful vocabulary. I found someone to give her elocution lessons. Now, she almost sounds like a proper young Home Counties girl. Trace of an accent. Misses the odd word. To cover her English shortcomings, she tells people she spent the first few years of her life in Guangzhou, just up from Hong Kong, and Nagoya, Japan, where her dad worked.

"Sorry," says Puppy, hunching her shoulders then dropping them with a sigh. "I'm good. Yeah, and doing okay. The coursework is too easy for me even with the joint degree. I get bored with it, but some folks struggle to keep up. A lot of stupid people at university. They don't really study or care about their subjects."

"You missed out on a lot of formal education, so you're not bored with the idea of learning things."

"Huh! Might be. I read a lot outside my subjects, too. I'm always reading! Even my friends think it's weird how much I read. And that stupid Jenny bitch is fucking Tylor again. Fuck, that girl has no taste!"

She has her little gang of friends. I get a warm, fuzzy feeling seeing her settled, but there's too brief a time to chat. I linger, soaking up and dishing gossip. She gives me that beautiful smile and tells me about the new room she has in the dorms this semester. Her 'daddy' sprung for a single, corner room.

We reach her car, a new-style Nissan Leaf in black, and I take off my jacket. She's going to act as my decoy this evening.

"Remember to strap the girls back this time," I remind her. "I'm not that prominent."

"What?" she asks, all mock-offended. "You don't like my party pillows?"

Ah, yes. This is our game we invented to help her expand her knowledge of English idioms. We compete to find many different phrases for things. "Your fruits of independence," I say. We have this whole thing where we try and make each other laugh.

"My nunga nungas."

"Your chesticles."

"Oh, I heard a new one on campus the other day. What was it? Oh! My jubblies!"

"That's not that new, sweetie. That's from Austin Powers."

"Oh, shid."

"Shit."

"Shit. Sorry. Right. ShiT. I sTill have Trouble with T."

Just this year, she started her university degree, part of which includes liaising between me, the faculty, and the student helpers I use on my larger commissions. Her double is chemistry and art, specifically the chemistry of paints, glazes, and historical artistic materials. Her ultimate goal is to scan a bunch of Roman statues then repaint them in their original colours. She's only seventeen, but I think she's mature beyond her years. Her birth certificate has her at eighteen, and she did amazingly well at her college exams last year. I was so proud!

She calls me and cries for an hour or so every few months, tells me about the nightmares that keep her awake. It doesn't look suspicious on my phone record that I get calls from the student who helps me with my projects. She also helps me dispose of the bodies. Puppy saw what the monster did to the men chasing her, and didn't even blink. Crawled right out of the bin where she hid, waited until I woke up, and introduced herself. Gave me some of her water.

"We'll have a proper hangout session tomorrow," I promise, handing her my phone. My pottery phone, not my burner phone. The phone's not made out of pottery, it's-

Whatever.

"Yeah, looking forward to it! I can show you my new dorm room! Oh, and you have to see what a mess the developers made of the cafeteria. It's just awful."

"Ha! Sounds fun." It's nice to have a friend I can talk to without having to hide too much. But even my little Puppy doesn't know the real truth about me.

I kiss her cheek then help her drape my coat over the dummy she has in the passenger seat. The flight case and my handbag come out of the suitcase. The suitcase goes in the trunk, regular clothes for a couple of days. I like the design of the old Leaf better. The funky shape was something that helped it stick out.

These days, everyone wants to blend in. I get it, but it's still boring.

Not having to pay the congestion charge around London is also a bonus. The new design is good, though. It's smaller, but feels bigger inside. Like the old Mini. That was a tiny car, but my dad could sit in the front of that and still have enough headroom to comb his hair. The whole CHADEMO thing puts me off, and the lack of liquid cooling for the battery limits the charging speed.

Which electric car do you think I should buy? It'll have to be second hand as I don't want to draw that much attention.

Anyway.

Wig, sunglasses, smear my lipstick at the corners, swap to a contrasting style of jacket. Puppy will dress in my clothes, with a wig and sunglasses, wander around the campus and dorms enough for people to see 'me' arrive, then tomorrow I'll start interviewing around midday. Once I'm back and I've had some sleep. She's got my walk down pat.

Mandarina Duck over one shoulder, I head back to the station, dissolutely rolling my nondescript flight-bag behind me, shuffling onto the three-forty to Godalming.

The journey is tedious.

Once clear of the station, I find my stolen boring-old-Corolla still where I parked it and throw my stuff in the back before carefully wending my way up to Buckinghamshire.

Rush-hour traffic. I don't mind the excess of cars. It makes mine more difficult to track, plus I don't need to be at my destination until late. I have a sandwich and a flask of coffee. The engine is quiet and pulls well. Even the CD player is up to date, so there's a jack for my burner-phone. Some wailing old Blues keeps me company along the way.

I do like modern music. I've been listening to The Black Keys. Dry My Soul by Amanda Jenssen caught my attention, plus the usual alt-pop. So few bands, nowadays. It's all artists with electronic backing tracks. It means the record companies don't have to hire a complex studio to record an album. They can do it all with one mic and a computer. I don't go to raves any more. Or whatever they call them these days. My electronic music is stuck on '90s Chemical Brothers and Barber Beats.

But there's just something about a rough old guy finger-picking a thumping tune on a guitar while he wails away. This is Mississippi Fred McDowell.

My dad really liked that stuff. We'd listen to it together while I 'helped' him out with the various carpentry projects he undertook to ruin the house. He could play them on the guitar, too. His versions were too-faithful copies of all the lyrics and music. Even Fred McDowell didn't play them exactly as they were on the album every time.

I came back to it when I inherited his records after- Well. After, after, after. There seems to be a lot of afters in my life. So it goes. The inevitability of things happening.

It's an acquired taste I picked up when I was young. I'm singing along, adding the lyrics the guitar sings. These were well-known songs in certain circles. At the time. So when he sings,

"You made me weep,

"And you made me moan,

"Well you caused me to leave my,

"My ha-a

And then the guitar sings, "appy home."

"But someday," guitar: "baby,"

"You ain't gonna worry my," guitar: "mind, any more."

Have you ever had that? Something in your life constantly worrying away at the back of your mind?

After I reach Buckinghamshire, I pull over and suction my burner-phone to the dash, waiting until the GPS comes on. Never start the GPS anywhere near your house. It's a dead give-away. I don't even take it out of Flight Mode until I'm at least in Godalming, Farnham, Petersfield, or some other large town.

I've tracked out a route that'll drop me more or less on the other side of the hill, and I can come to the cottage obliquely. Google maps satellite view. Useful.

My anticipation's rising. Hopefully, they'll be there, and I can get a clue. If not, I've got Bright-Eyes' licence plate. This is the fun part. Hunting my prey. I'll find them. Like poor, deluded Dan said, luck always runs out.

I flirt with Swan Bottom and Lee Clump, but take care to circle larger villages when I can. It's still early enough for the roads to be busy and I pass as just another commuter coming home.

Oh, look. Local riding club. I was thinking of joining mine, but a horse requires way too much upkeep. I'm never there.

The farm lane I wanted to use turns out to be a cul-de-sac with four huge commuter-mansions in spacious grounds. Damn. That wasn't on street-view. A recent development.

Last thing I want to do is panic the new landed gentry of bored, curtain-twitchers. A snort of frustration and I roll past a mile or so, pull up in a field gateway, kill the engine, un-stick my burner. I'm reading CJ Cherryh's *Morgaine* series. I'm onto the second book, *Well of Shiuan*, and it's getting to the interesting part where we find out the identity of the mysterious swordsman who befriended the peasant girl.

Seriously, how awesome are mobile phones these days? I can read books, listen to music, take photos, navigate, all on a cheap burner. You young murderers don't know how lucky you are.

I crack a window to stop them misting, sip my coffee and become absorbed. There's a cluster of cars every minute, then every ten minutes, then every half an hour, then nothing.

I'm not that tired. I did have a little snooze earlier today, remember? Reaching the end of a chapter I have to force myself to look up. Yeah, it's about time.

I slip out and take care of business behind the hedge. Too much coffee. I get a pretty good stream when I have to squat. I know Puppy has a regular sprinkler system down there. She can barely keep her piss contained when she has a toilet. I wonder if it has anything to do with all the things she's had shoved up her over the years?

She told me about this one time some Yakuza youngsters got drunk, stuck a gun up her cunt, another up her arse, and played Russian roulette for a couple of clicks, before the boss came in and made them stop. She was so resigned to death by that point she didn't care if they killed her. This was before the boss' son took an interest. He seemed to genuinely care about her, but mostly just wanted to tie her up so he could slap her around and feel all dominant.

I'm getting sidetracked. Again. I do that a lot. You've probably noticed.

Anyway.

My car turns easily in the gateway, then trundles gently back to my start point with the lights off. The commuter mansions are all still and dark; brooding carbuncles with motion sensors and high-security, automatic gates. Engine off. I roll backwards, *reverse*, down the lane. I stay well clear of the first gate but still far enough from the road that I look like I'm visiting. Hopefully, being a cul-de-sac, no-one will look closely on the off chance they do pass by.

You can't park reliably at the side of a country road, regardless of how late it is. The amount of traffic at all hours these days, no matter how remote. Yeesh. It only needs to go wrong once. Well, twice.

In the morning, I'll wait for the early rush hour a country address usually hosts, then merge in with the rest of the London commuters. But first, let's do this.

Almost bouncing with excitement, I unpack my gear. I'm not taking my entire handbag, just what I'll need right now. Both hands free will be better. Lockpicks, in case I have to bother with subtlety; compact binoculars, because knowing is half the battle; knife, because I want this to be quiet; spectrum-analysing RF detector, because being caught by a hidden camera is a pain. Also, my phone, because I can record information, look things up and all the other wonderful things a mobile phone can do. Bright-Eyes was making a call to 'ma'am', so my carrier should cover it. Zip-tie handcuffs, tags, plastic bags, you get the idea.

Fortunately, there's a fashion niche for camo-pants with cargo-pockets on the side. Combine that with a beige tank-top and a red jacket, into which I've sewn a camouflage lining. My hair is contained by a black headband with green patches that unrolls and covers my face. All good. I've always liked having shorter hair but girls can get away with any fashion accessory when talking to policemen. They never even think to ask why I need a headband with my hairstyle.

Even these boots suit the look.

I reverse the jacket, unroll my headband. It has eye-holes hidden in the folds.

Ready to go.

While waiting for my night-vision I spend a couple of minutes scanning the tree-line with the binoculars, looking for glints. It's cloudier than it was the last time I was here. I can't see anyone in the dark.

The cul-de-sac is flanked and backed by empty fields. The trees don't start until about two-hundred metres past the houses. The hill-line peaks about a hundred metres beyond that. The field is freshly ploughed, that rich smell of turned earth, which would be a muddy pain if I wasn't planning to stick to the hedgerows.

A little shiver of excitement. This is it. The thrill of not being a housewife. Not stuck in some meaningless nine to five. My pulse rises but even that is a reminder of why I do this.

Seriously. How do I function? It's insane to even think about it.

The clues I find will inevitably lead to the other part. The part I'm less thrilled about but most addicted to. The monster. The blood. Heaving dead bodies about while bits of them go squish and squirt blood and other stuff all down the front of your dress.

Oh, wow, no, for real. There was this one time where this guy had no pants on, and seriously, he must have been eating pure fibre because the shit that came out of his arse was almost liquid. I'd just bought these new Calvin Klein jeans and all the little chunks of crap worked their way right in. To cut a long story short, that was when I started getting my 'work' outfits from charity bins.

Is that too much information? Should I pan tastefully to the wafting curtains or linger on the fluids? Which would you prefer?

I slip over the gate, gloves on this time, into the field at one side and just flat out sprint.

It would be nice to have a couple of unbeatable Olympic records to my name.

A chill of night air in my lungs and I arrive, panting, at the messy trees. The hill is steeper on this side. I track carefully until I spy a mud trail leading in. Either a game trail or a hiker's path. I check the heights and it seems clear. Backing up a couple of paces, I launch a good fifteen metres before the path begins and land maybe three metres in. I didn't notice any sensors or tripwires on the path entrance, but it's better to be safe than sorry.

That knee twinges an early warning. I crouch to give it a bit of a stretch and enjoy the sensation. I'm enjoying it a bit too much and have to pull myself back. Last thing I need is to twist my dodgy knee, freak out and kill everyone.

I scope the forest from my new vantage point. Still nothing. Are they not watching this side of the hill? Careless. If Deluded Dan said anything about the exploits of my 'mother' they apparently didn't believe him. Or they abandoned the house. Or they thought he was exaggerating. Well, let's go find out.

I reach the hill-crest and lie flat, easing my way over the rich-smelling earth, past a tangle of brambles and bushes. Making a fist, I lie the binoculars on top and start a careful sweep.

Nothing.

Hang on, where's the cottage? Oh, all the way back to my left. The cluster of high evergreens surrounds an ugly clump of dilapidation. I can't hear the faint hum of the generator from here.

Remote curtains glow. Someone's home.

My distances were off. It looks like that might be to my advantage. They have a high spotter, propped just under the hill-crest, tree at his back so he won't show a silhouette, bush in front to break up his shape. From the side, though, he's kind of obvious.

That tree's going to make things awkward. It's always hard to judge these things. I get over-excited and jump too far, or pull back too much and land short. Gives them time to scream. He shifts for comfort and adjusts the position of something that sinks my heart.

A rifle.

Fuck.

That's a big fucking gun.

Is that a Bushmaster or something? Fucking assault rifle! In the UK? I hate guns. I'm not fast enough to dodge a fucking bullet. Shit. I should have brought my gun. I have a silencer. But this is recon, not wetwork. Maybe everyone's in the cottage, and it's just the one watcher. It's been a couple of days. How much of a guard are they going to have after a couple of days?

Huh. Silencer's the wrong fucking word. They don't make a gun silent. Nowadays they call them 'suppressors' so there's no confusion. And that FN57 is LOUD.

Okay. No need to panic just yet. I continue the scan. The tiny parabolic dish on the RF scanner doesn't pick up any noise except from the generator, and a ping from Watcher, so he probably has a radio.

No cameras.

The binoculars tell me there's a strange clump of bushes, artificial looking, down near the fence at the front. Might be a man there as well. All with Big Black Guns? No RF ping. Empty nest? Or no radio?

Shit, shit, shit.

It's almost impossible to take out a guard silently in a situation like this. The woods are lovely, dark and deep and all, but quiet. That damned fancy, new generator isn't audible even from where he's sitting. Creeping up on this guy will be impossible. There's no clear path to him. He's surrounded by vines. Leaves. Clever.

Even with my strength and speed, the sound of taking someone down will alert the front watcher, if not the whole the cabin. Thrashing. A muted scream. That'll carry on a night like this. Without the possibility of background noise, it's going to be blind luck if I don't get everyone converging on my sorry arse in ten seconds.

But they're still here. They're waiting for me. I can get information. If I can get Watcher, there's every chance I can make it to the house, pick up something useful from their chatter, plant the bugs, put trackers on their cars. They'll panic when they find the body. Panic means too much talking and undisciplined actions, so this could be a veritable gold mine that leads me right to my prey.

Or, this might get very, very messy. Very, very quickly.

I sidle closer. There's a clearer patch that'll enable me to step down for a better angle. I throw a rock way on the other side. Watcher turns casually, almost bored. I do the stepping thing, but then the Watcher does the professional thing of also checking the other way. Straight at me. I might be fucked already. He blinks, and that's about as long as it takes for me to spring.

Too high! Dammit!

Fortunately, it takes him a second to register the fact that there's a woman flying at him.

The rifle comes up. One hand goes to the radio but then goes to the gun. That twitch of indecision saves me. I hook over like a cat startled by a cucumber, lash out with my boot and catch him hard, feeling the skull give way. There's an audible crunch. I land as lightly as I can, but still way too much crashing through the forest floor, without him to absorb my impact. Bad angle on the hit and the landing. That knee sings at me and I feel way too much of the sun.

That glorious fire!

Oh, if I pop-off because of that fucking knee I will be so upset. Focus.

He's slipping sideways, scraping noisily against the tree. I spring back to catch him before he thumps to the crunching ground, crumpling him into a foetal position behind the bush. My knife goes into the downward side of his neck, so he bleeds onto the ground instead of spraying all over me. He's unconscious already. Possibly dead already, but it's best to be sure.

Ew. Warm and sticky.

I wipe my black, latex glove on his shirt, trying to get rid of the heat on the rubber, holding him down in case he wakes up before he dies. They do that sometimes. Spasm awake. Like when you dream you're falling and jerk back to the real world. Except they're not dreaming and actually dying. But no, he stays down. This is how you build a terrifying reputation. Kill everyone who witnesses your fuck ups.

Nothing.

Nobody moves around the house. That clump of bushes stays still. The high hedges hide what's happening inside, but even on this quiet night, I can't hear a thing.

Except. I can. Sort of. Raised voices inside the cottage. Is that what's distracting them from keeping proper contact with the watch? It's not a knock-down, drag-out, screaming argument, but definitely speaking in anger. Did one of the girls misbehave?

There it is again. A man. An angry man.

I can't make out anything being said. It's all muffled like Charlie Brown adult speak.

The guy whose neck I'm kneeling on bleeds out enough that he won't wake up, ever.

My victim had some serious gear. Webbing on the jacket contains a good knife. I should have killed him with his own knife! Ah! Missed opportunity. Earbud to a walkie that isn't from Maplins. This fucking gun is like a HK416, or some modern take on the M16. I'm not up on the new wave of assault rifles. I prefer a bullpup. This thing has IR laser sights, a suppressor, and weighs less than a chicken dinner.

Ex-military guards with this kind of equipment? That's a level above even my usual prey. Normally, it's clumsy little circles of elite wankers who can't imagine anything bad happening to them that money won't fix. They have great secrecy, but rarely this level of heavy-hitters.

Watcher starts his death rattle, gurgling and twitching. My stomach gurgles right along and I swallow hard. Mercifully, it's over quickly and I find myself obsessively rubbing blood off my knife against his sleeve as I try to plot my next move.

I made noise. This wasn't a silent take-down, but the radio hasn't crackled, no-one moved. There might still be someone at the front.

They could have a van load of people waiting to roll in.

Shit.

I can probably make it to house unseen. Jump the high hedge on that blind-side, next to the generator shed, land quietly on what passes for a back lawn, overgrown, but still softer and silenter than the forest floor. At the very least, I've cleared myself an escape path.

Besides, I really want to know what all the shouting is about.

I finish wiping my knife, carefully stow it. Maybe I should grab the big gun? No. I want information, not blood.

It's easy to get down to the fence. The trees that hide them from me also hide me from them. There's probably a Chinese proverb about that.

That suspicious clump of bushes at the front is an artificial hide, but nobody's home. I count my blessings, or curses, and slip back along the hedge until I reach the blind side of the cottage.

After my last almost-disaster I try to settle into a simple leap. The adrenalin from worrying if I'll overshoot is making me so jacked up I'm likely to overshoot. In the end, I commit to an effort, and just clear the tips of the pines. I land and roll. That dodgy knee of mine twinges hard and I almost lose myself to a wave of ecstasy.

Seriously? My fucking hair and nails still grow, but that torn tendon isn't going to mend? Oh, my holy fuck. The joy tingles along my nerves releasing that velvet-electric wash of ecstasy.

No, no, no.

Not now.

Just fucking calm the fuck down.

I try to connect to the world. The low thrum of the generator, the smell of the dank cottage, moonlight on the clouds. That voice. There's a voice. I want to hear what the voice has to say. I really, really want to know.

Sneaking closer, I keep my pleasure at a manageable throb. Even the sneaking brings twinges. I am so close to losing it completely.

"I mean, where the fuck did you think we was goin' all them times, Danny boy? Do you really think there were, like, full on brothels an' shit IN THE MIDDLE OF A FUCKIN' WAR ZONE?"

"It wasn't a warzone! It was a city!"

"Jesus fuckin' Christ! No wonder you only lasted one fuckin' tour!"

It's Deluded Dan! I rub the knee to ease it down. Please! I really want to see poor Deluded Dan. Please, please, please. That focus drags me back from the joy, the rapturous, amazing connection to the sun. Oh, you can never know how good it feels!

No. Dan. Detective Daniel Ripplewater. Wait. What the fuck is he even doing here?

"The whole time I was over there I didn't know what was right, what was wrong," says Dan. "Half the stuff we had to do..." The rest is too quiet. Come on, Dan! Speak up!

"And now you know? Fuck off! You don't know shit!"

Wait. I don't think that's Bright-Eyes. The accent is all South London.

I stand, flex the knee a couple of times and slip over to the window. No. I'll hear better from the ill-fitted door. Oh, awesome. It's one of those stable-doors, and the damp-twisted top half doesn't fit on the bottom any-more. There's a gap.

"Now I can find out! I'm a detective! I can detect, get the right information. Find stuff."

"So you had to go pokin' around 'ere. And you got the wrong information! We're not part of that Birmingham mob. We work for someone else. It's not-"

"Who?! Who the fuck do you work for?" Yeah, tell us who you work for, London. Make my life easier, why don't you?

"Mate, you should've just done what we asked and gone about yer merry. Run the fuckin' fingerprints and handed over the fuckin' file." Dammit! Bad guys never soliloquise properly in real life. "But no, your little dick wanted to go all the way down to fuckin' Godalming and visit the cute little artist-girl."

"She's not involved!"

"Oh, you big fuckin' hero. I know she's not involved, you twat! I read the fuckin' file! I didn't have to go all the way down there to work out she's not fuckin' involved! And if you hadn't followed your dick half-way across the fuckin' country, got all suspicious after your little chat, and poked about in NONE OF YOUR FUCKIN' BUSINESS, I wouldn't be 'ere workin' meself up to killin' a stupid fuck like you!"

Kill him? Oh. That's, er, unfortunate. The temptation to try and peer through the crack in the door is too much. Wait. Do I really want to watch? I bend down, shifting my weight, and that knee twinges again! Oh, yes! Oh, fuck yes! If I release to this, the daemon might save Dan.

No! No, no, no.

I can't let myself care about some fucking bastard cop. Deluded and righteous as he may be. With nice hair.

"Go on then! Fucking kill me! Put your gun in my face and pull the fucking trigger!"

Wait. No. This is not good.

Through the crack I see London lift his gun, "Oh, you stupid fuckin' cunt."

# 7

# Interior

I wake slowly, stretching on the mattress. Mattress? Oh, thank fuck. I'm waking up in my own bed. It's the middle of the night, but it's probably because I need a piss instead of the usual reason I wake in the middle of the night.

No. I took care of that already, behind the hedge.

Is that someone knocking? I had this nice dream of... What the fuck was it? Dan. Detective Dan and I were doing the washing up, cleaning those baking trays of burnt muffin, him with his top off, me splashing water and suds onto his glistening chest. Only, we had a bit of trouble getting the trays properly clean because of the blood he kept leaking onto them. I was teasing him about it. When was the last time I cleaned these damned blankets? They smell a bit funky.

There's that knocking again. I should check the door. Wait. It's not a knocking at a door. Blankets? I'm lying on top of a rough, course blanket. Army grey. Oh, shit.

This isn't my fucking bed.

Oh, for fucks sake.

Can't I please just stay asleep a little longer and dream of topless detectives? Who the fuck keeps knocking like that? I squeeze my eyes tighter. Not again. I never want to wake like this ever again. Tears already sting. Something else on my face. I wipe at it, half asleep, but my hand is damp and sticky.

Fuck no! Oh, fuck, no!

I lift my arm and bury my face in my armpit, sobbing quietly onto the pillow, hiding from the light. I hate this. Hate that this is of my life; waking in strange places with stuff all over me.

The tears are flowing, my breath comes in sad little sobs like I'm nine and my hamster died all over again. I'm like one of those fucking drug-addicted whores I keep running across. Those hopeless cases trying to punish themselves for all their bad choices by making even worse choices.

Shit.

I keep wiping, wanting to be clean. No, that's not my face. It's soaked into this stupid mask thing I'm wearing! Why the fuck did I think this was clever? I just look like a fucking moron with this stupid thing over my face! Why do I think anything I do is clever or useful or has any fucking point to it at all? I sit up and rip off the mask in frustration, feeling horrifically horrible. Beyond crying, swamped by utter despair, tears streaming down my face, chest convulsing, gasping wildly at the air.

How is this even possible? How can my body even do this?

Oh, fuck. I lean over the side of the bed and a stream of vomit burns my throat on its way to the floor.

My favourite term for that I discovered when I was living in Australia. Chunder. The technicolour yodel, if you've got the time to say it. I spit out some of the sandwich and coffee that are still in my mouth. Oh, yeah. Puppy came up with, 'Driving the porcelain bus', as part of our game. That's another good one, though it mostly refers to throwing up into a toilet.

There's a mug with some water beside the bed. I always put some there, though I can't for the life of me remember why. I wake and there's a glass of water. Mostly.

I plan these. Mostly. Time my hunts so I come around with plenty of night left to clean up and have a few sips of water.

This was not planned.

Oh, fuck, this is an unholy mess. I take a sip and immediately spit it out. Note to self, remember to wash the cup when you're coming down from your murderous fit of ecstasy.

What's the line from *Buffy*? My life does, on occasion, suck beyond the telling of it. Are pop-culture references better than literary quotes, or basically the same thing? Am I just trying to sound cooler off the back of someone else's genius?

Okay. Feeling slightly less suicidal. Some slower breaths and I'm a little more together. With shaking hands, I undo the zipper on my jacket and use the top underneath to clean some of the mess off my face. The dampness from the tears helps. I sniff a few times to clear my nose, then wipe that last. I pull my top down, and with the exaggerated care you use when picking up someone else's snotty tissue, I do the jacket back up, scanning the room, trying not to look at anything on the floor.

"Oh, shit! It's you!"

I startle and see... DAN! It's good ol' Dopey Detective Dan, tied to a chair and completely freaked out. I didn't kill him! Oh, thank fucking Christ for that. Oh, wait. He's seen my face. That means I'm probably going to have to kill him now.

Shit.

Shouldn't have named him.

He was the one knocking? How could he knock when he's tied to a chair? No, wait. He was shuffling the chair towards his mate, looking for a knife to cut himself free. The man with the London accent is... In several different places. I'm not going to look at that. My gag reflex twitches again.

"What on Earth...?" Dan is very upset. "How can it be you?"

"Shut the fuck up!" I really don't want to deal with this right now. The drab, little cottage-one-room has two beds. Cheap, pine-frame singles with army blankets and sheets that used to be white. The tiny kitchen juts out at the back, making for a sort of afterthought on one corner. The toilet is that outhouse in the back garden. There's a couch near the front door, propping up someone's disembodied arm. Oh, fuck. A laminated table with a wallet and keys, surrounded by metal-framed chairs, one of which contains Dan. And blood. Blood. So much fucking blood. Oh, fuck me sideways.

"Look, just untie me and I'm sure we can sort this all out."

"I said, shut the fuck up!"

I throw the gore-dampened headband at him. It slaps into his face and sticks. He flinches, shaking his head about trying to dislodge it. And he shuts the fuck up.

I've always been good at throwing things. Tantrums, snowballs, rocks, bloodied tampons. If you ever want to dump a boy real quick, yank aside your panties, pull out your soaking crotch swab while he watches, and slap him right across the face with it. You'll never see him again, I guarantee.

With a sigh, I slough of the bed and shuffle across the syrupy floor towards the kitchen. You know that thing where you've just had a disappointing fuck and need to wash up but you're not in the mood to coddle his precious fucking ego? Yeah, that.

It's always a good idea, in these situations, not to look down to see what you've just stepped in.

I feel like crap, right now. This is why I have all these people singing me the Blues, people who can understand what it is to feel this low. It's why I've never really liked Robert Johnson. Sure, he could play and his voice had a nice quality about it, but I always felt as though he was enjoying himself too much.

There's a hand-pump attached to the side of the sink. Probably a rainwater tank in the roof. Or maybe it's connected to a deep well. I work the lever and dank, dirty water flows.

OH FUggkkk! A huge convulsion runs through, leaving me shaking, clinging to the sink, mouth open in gibbering horror at the thing that took over me.

Breathe.

I just lean there and breathe for a while, wondering if this is going to end me. Wanting it to end me. But no. A few breaths later and I'm still alive.

Okay. Pump handle. I touched the fucking pump handle. The sink. And the edge of the bed when I leaned over. My gloves are shredded. They're not meant for that level of abuse. A bracelet of black rubber is all that remains around one wrist. I'm going to have to remember all the hard surfaces I touched, so I don't leave a fingerprint anywhere.

You'd be amazed at how much forensic information they can get from the scene of a fire.

Water on my face just starts to make me feel sad again. I find myself sniffling, a catch in my breath that comes before crying. I look up. Water runs down my neck. Fuck. Now my bra is going to be all wet and uncomfortable. I hate it when that happens.

The ceiling displays a disgusting mix of grease stains over the stove, blackened mildew in the corners. Look up, if you ever feel like crying. It's a physiology thing. It's harder to start crying if your eyes are rolled up.

Some deeper breaths and I'm back in control again.

Control. Ha! There's a fucking joke.

I glance back at the bloodied mess to remind myself exactly how much fucking control I have. There are bits in the little pools of blood. Chunks of flesh and organs and brains. Lovely.

None of them are going to be able to tell me a fucking thing, now. Why can't anything ever go right for me?

More water. And onto my hair, cooling my head. There's a stack of clean tea-towels in one drawer, with a faint, musty odour about them. (Drawer knobs. I touched the drawer knobs.) It doesn't look as though anyone has used them since they were put there. I peel one from the middle. Probably cleanest.

"What the fuck did you do that for? Hello?"

Oh, FUCK! I really don't want to have to think about poor Dan right now. He thinks this narrative is about him, and wants some attention. Little sook.

I step back over to the doorway and lean there, drying my face and hair, wiping as much of the blood off the rest of me as possible. There's not that much. Mostly just a few heavy spurts, a lot of spray.

Dan is momentarily silenced by the sight of me casually cleaning myself. If he sees how fucked-up I really am... I wipe and rub and scrub, scanning the room out of the corner of my eye because I don't want to have to look directly at what I, at what the beast did.

It wasn't me. It was something inside me that enjoys tearing up this type of person. Not me.

"So." I lock eyes with Dan. "You're in this mess because you liked the look of my arse. I didn't think there was a full-length photo of me in that file. I fucked the last policeman they sent to make sure he took it out."

Dan stares at me, not sure what's going on, unable to reconcile the figure before him with the bumbling domestic from the village. He tries to wipe the blood off his own face on one shoulder, but his hands have been expertly tied. London knew his business.

The accented killer is lying to one side of the room, stomach bloated from internal bleeding. His face looks like he died screaming in pain, so I can make as much noise as I like.

How long was I asleep? Ten minutes or so, judging by the lack of general congealment. Fifteen at the outside. That's about average for one of my episodes.

Three other men lie dead, scattered about like discarded toys after a vicious sibling argument. At least one of them is missing an arm. I get a sudden flash of the bone cracking as it left the socket, sending a jolt of revulsion through me.

I really don't want to be thinking about what I, no. What the monster did. It's easier if I think of them as broken GI Joe dolls. Blame some daemon. Don't name them.

"There was only one photo in the file," Dan says cautiously. "It made you seem all mysterious. I found one on-line, though."

"Like fuck you did! Where was it?"

"On the gallery website, from Godalming, an old exhibition."

"Oh, that fucking Malvisi bitch! I fuckin' told her. Shit." I kick London's foot in frustration. "I'll have to get onto that. Thanks."

A spluttered cough and both of us look at London. Fuck! Not dead? Dan calls out his name and I deliberately block it out. Don't want to know his real name. I'm calling him London. Because of the accent.

I squat, keeping some distance in case he coughs something nasty over me. This might not be quite the unholy fucking mess that it looks like right now. His eyes flicker, unfocused, at weird angles. I slide closer, ready to spring away. I think we're past the faking-it-and-suddenly-lunging stage with London.

"We're in the cottage, mate," I tell him, loud enough to get his attention. "Do you recognise the cottage?" If I can get his eyes to focus, I might be able to get some sense out of him. "Can you understand me? This is the cottage. Do you know who owns the cottage?"

The eyes even out, blink a few times, but he can't seem to settle onto a detail until he catches a glimpse of my face. Then he gets that confused look I'm so used to seeing. "You!" he whispers. A dark humour passes over his slack features. "Oh, you have no idea what The Lady is going to do to you for this."

"The Lady? You call her, Ma'am, yes? Is she the one that owns this cottage?"

"Owns...? Nah, we just borrow it when," cough, "when we found a girl and need to keep her for... It's- Wait. She's... She ain't here! She got away! The girl got away!"

He looks around the room in a panic, but that causes movement, which tweaks his broken spine. London spasms, coughing, and I slide back out of the way.

So even tracing ownership of this place isn't going to get me anywhere. Shit on a brick. The Range Rover's probably also a lease. The bloated wreck is screaming and rattling and choking. There's nothing more he can tell me now.

I stay down, tea-towel pressed over my eyes, using the warmth and darkness to keep myself from cracking completely. Not in front of Dan, who starts shouting his ex-friend's name over and over.

La, la, la! Not listening!

I move the flannel mask a little away and stare sidelong at the detective from under a heavy brow. Well, yeah. Let's talk about poor Dan, shall we?

"Jesus, he's dead?" Dan sounds genuinely sad that the man who was about to murder him has now finished noisily expiring. "You just kicked him once. How the hell did you *do* that? I mean..." Dan turns to look at another victim over by the door. "You jumped right across the room. You, you just tore them apart! What the fuck was that?"

"I study Kung-Fu," I mutter into the towelling.

"Kung-Fu? Are you serious? What fucking Kung-Fu?"

I let the towel drop, staring up. "Mostly softer styles, Taijiquan, Xingyi-"

"Tai Chi? What? Like old people do in the park?"

"Yeah. If you understand the applications behind the moves, it's one of the most brutally effective forms of fighting ever devised. And some BaGua, Tien-Tai."

"Baa what?"

"Ba Gua Zhan. The Eight Tri-gram Palm. Circle boxing." I stand and pace about. I find it helps if I don't stand still for too long when I'm making up bullshit. "I studied in China with real masters. All the proper, secret Shaolin temple stuff."

What? He might be stupid enough to buy that. It's the best I could do at short notice. And if he does believe me, he gets to live.

"Studied for how long? Since you were six or something? You kicked," he uses London's name again and I turn away, blinking, blotting it from my memory, "so hard you broke his spine. From the front!"

"Really? Oh, is that why that happens? I've always wondered how I manage that one."

"What? What the fuck is that supposed to mean? You tell me what the fuck is-" He jerks in his chair, but they did a great job of restraining him. "Fucking untie me! Now!"

I stalk across the room and grab his face. "You're not giving me orders, soldier. Your rank means nothing here. Military, police, nothing. You want to know what's going on?" I wait, but the confusion is stopping him from hearing properly. I lean down to his level and speak plainer, quieter, making it an actual question. "Do you want to know what's happening right now?" He nods as much as my grip allows. "I'm trying to decide if I should kill you or not."

A spark of anger enters his eyes, that self-righteous arrogance that gives him his confidence, the little swagger in his step you sometimes see in ex-military. But to his credit, it's just a flash, a mayfly of machismo. Once it's gone, he genuinely doesn't know what to say.

Or is it that he hasn't had any training in hostage negotiation?

Is everything about him just professionalism, just the training? Institutionalised from school to the army to the police. Everything ranked and ordered, everyone knowing who to listen to and obey. Only allowed his self expression within the rules. Stretch conformity but never tear it. Where's the real Dan?

"You've seen me, Danny boy. In all my glory. And I don't leave witnesses." Except when it's convenient for spreading disinformation. Or someone nobody will believe. Or it's someone I can almost trust. Like Puppy. Can I trust Dan? Oh, shit, I really don't think I could kill him straight. Not right now. I'm barely together enough to have this conversation.

"Are you going to put your foot through my fucking head as well?" he asks, glancing at a corpse to one side.

I look over. Sure enough, a ragged hole about the size of my boot hollows out the side of that one's head. The skin tore aside, the skull caved in sharply, cutting all three of the meninges, the membranes that surround the brain. The grey goop leaking out looks like burnt cherry blancmange over-flowing a spoon. There are lumps of it on the floor.

I go all light-headed, turn randomly and walk over to a wall, leaning there gasping for a steady breath, both hands high on the plaster, looking down at a relatively clean patch of old carpet. I think it might have been blue once.

Wall. I touched the wall. I'll have to remember to wipe it down.

"What the fuck is wrong with you?" Dan asks. "Now you're squeamish? Now? You pulled that guy's arm clean off, but now you suddenly can't bear to look at him?" I am so going to kill him. "And how the hell did you do that? You don't have any upper-body strength at all."

"Oh, Dan, Dan. It's not all about strength. Or didn't your military training teach you anything about technique? I lock my arms in the mechanically correct position and push with both my legs. I don't use my upper body. It's all in the legs. Helps if you kick through the joint and dislocate it first. Besides. I have some strength. I lift those pots and bags of wet clay around all day, remember?"

Again, he's blank. Then, overnight, a forest grows. His rod-straight spine relaxes, and he accepts what he saw. Well, technically he rejects what he actually saw, and accepts the most logical explanation. I am Kung-Fu master, super-killer extraordinaire.

The human mind is weird.

"It's just hard to, to believe. You're the same as your mother, then? She used to kill people like that. From what little there is in the file. Did she train you, like in secret or something?"

That sounds good. Let's go with that. "Yeah, she'd visit me in Australia and China. On and off."

"China?"

"I went twice a year for two months. Missed loads of school, but I trained with these old weirdos out in Henan, just down from Denfeng, near the old Little-Forest Temple."

"Little Forest?"

"Shao Lin. Little Forest. The Temple's a tourist trap, nowadays, but there are places in the hills where Triads always had their own schools, and old Masters still train the proper stuff."

"Your mother left you with the Triads? She wasn't killing them, too?"

"Triads are the old anti-government gangs. Heroes of the Marsh? No? The Chinese government has a habit of wiping out the Shaolin Temples every couple of hundred years. The monks have a well-established network of underground connections. The hardcore, criminal Triad gangs grew out of that, but mostly the gangs were about helping poor country folks. Robin Hood was in a gang. History is different from what you pick up off the TV. You need to travel more, Dan. Get the first-hand, word-of-mouth distortions, not just the government-sponsored distortions."

"Seems like your mother had very specific plans for you."

"Nah. She let me choose my own path. Just wanted me to be safe. I came to this mainly to track down the men who killed her. I get the same rage fits as her, where I lose track of my actions. Instinct just takes over, and my instincts are highly trained." I look meaningfully at the bodies. Dan frowns, following my gaze. "And then," I gesture to the bed, "I wake up."

"Like, what? A Berserker or something? Are you saying you're a Berserker?"

"Probably, yeah. I can, sort of, trigger them now, though. I still don't have any control. Can't remember anything from when I'm in that state. You're lucky I didn't kill you. Maybe because you were tied to the chair, I didn't register you as a threat."

Rage fits? That's as close to the truth as I can get with someone who doesn't really know what's going on. He'll be suspicious, so let's give him an old memory. Something he can check up on.

"The first time I actually killed someone I was like…" Hang on, how old am I pretending to be, now? Quick bit of maths. "Seventeen."

"Seventeen!"

"Yep. Just a kid. My mum tracked a gang of child molesters to some seaside cottage near Walberswick, back down towards Dunwich. They caught and killed her. She'd send me postcards coding the location of any bad guys she found, then another to confirm she'd killed them. I didn't get the second postcard. I found the gang and nearly got killed myself. Thankfully, it was only half a dozen old men. One of them must have got lucky when mother came calling. I never found her body. Probably sunk in the ocean. They thought I was just some kid when they caught me easily enough. I got angry with myself, angry at them, and blanked out. I woke up and they were all dead. It was really messy. Well, look around. I didn't even have an alibi for that one."

That's all bullshit as well, of course. I was very much into my stride by the time I committed the Dunwich horror. The story did make the papers though, 'Murder Suicide in Seaside Paradise'.

"And you have an alibi for this? Now?"

"Yeah. I'm in London. Well, my phone is, anyway. A friend of mine used it earlier this evening, took some geo-tagged and dated photos, then she 'grammed from my account. Don't worry, I've trained her well. She checks the background carefully for any reflective surfaces or identifiable witnesses. So, yeah, then I burnt the cottage in Dunwich to the ground, just like I'm going to do here, and that was that."

"You're going to burn the cottage? What? Siphon some petrol from the car?"

I stare at him a while. I mean, it's not like he's used to this, so I guess that's not a bad suggestion for a first timer. Not that I'm going to let him know that.

"Generator, dummy. The place is powered by a very expensive, almost-silent generator. Knowing the military efficiency of this bunch, there's half a year's supply of fuel for it in that lean-to with the toilet."

"Diesel doesn't burn that well, you know."

"If it was a diesel generator, it wouldn't be that quiet, dummy."

"Oh. Right, right." He looks around, not even that offended that I called him dummy. Promising. I thought he might be too used to giving orders to take any. He has this strange little half-smile when he says, "So, now you hunt down pimps?"

And I want more than anything to trust that smile, to trust that quirky, not too funny, nice hair. Fuck.

"Oh, no, no, no. After that first time, I stopped. Didn't want anything more to do with it. Except, now and then, I get wind of a particularly bad bunch. I've got my mum's email, and all that. Her old informants still send her stuff. You know what kind of men these people were. Even that man you thought was your friend."

"He wasn't involved with this lot. You heard him."

"Yeah, I heard. I also heard what he was telling you about his time overseas. You didn't partake in any of his rape parties, did you? Hunting down some local girls for a weekend of illegal imprisonment and molestation. Didn't even know about them, from what he was saying. But I think he's involved in something far worse."

The kind of people who really interested me. My true prey, slipping through my fingers after this fuck-up.

"He was still my friend," Dan insists, sullen at his own naivety.

"Sure. Right. He was going to shoot you in the face."

"He was still my friend. You wouldn't understand. It's a military thing. Guys you've served with, fought next to. That bond can't be broken."

"Yeah, I've heard all that war-glamorising bullshit before. 'It's about the man beside you!' fucking trauma-response-driven crap."

"It's not bullshit!" Dan jerks against his restraints, the half-smile gone. Is this the real man? How can we really know what people will do in the most extreme of circumstances? He takes a couple of breaths and asks, quite reasonably, "Look, could you please just untie me?"

"Why? So you can over-power me in my weakened state, and escape?"

"Nah, it's just that you're the second person who's threatened to kill me while I've been tied to this chair. I thought maybe you could tape me to the couch. For a bit of variety."

Ha! See? Now that he's settled down, he's falling back into his humour and quirkiness. But is that the real him? Ugh. I am so fucking confused right now!

I pull out my knife, walking slowly back towards him. He's a soldier, used to stressful situations, stays still and quiet. Maybe that's why the beast didn't notice him tied to the chair. How calm is he? Is this another act? I place the tip of the knife against his jugular, holding it lightly enough that I can feel the faint pulse vibrating up the blade.

"They're going to be hunting you, too, now. Dan. As well as my 'mother'." I make sure to pronounce the quotation marks. "I could help you. Find them. Bring them to justice."

"I think we might have different ideas about the meaning of the word 'justice'."

"Quite the ideologist, aren't we? It's not like you can arrest them, Dan. This Ma'am your friends report to? She has men at her command, and a lot of money to buy information. Did you see the guns these 'private security contractors' were carrying? You won't get near her before they track you off somewhere and kill you, like they almost did tonight. I can help you get clear in a way that none of it can touch you ever again."

"And what do you get out of this deal? A way sate your blood-lust?"

I allow my revulsion at that remark to show in my face.

"I'm sorry," he apologises.

I'm not sure why he's sorry. That's the rub. Is this a game of self-preservation? Does he actually care, or did he just drop the attitude and go all apologetic, like I do? His pulse is steady through the blade. His eyes are evasive. "I didn't mean that. I just... I'm a bit freaked out by this whole situation. We might be able to do a, er, mutually satisfactory, ah, thing..."

Quirky. Funny. Act?

"Sure, I understand. Girl you had a crush on turns out to be a psycho. It happens. But hey now." I smile coyly. "I'm sure I can think of something you can do for me." I carefully lift the knife away. "Tell you what. I'm going to get some petrol. Then I'll spend a good half hour cleaning this place and wiping my girlie footprints off the floor. Then I'll set it up to burn. That'll give me time to decide if I untie you from that chair before I light the match."

# 8
## Car

When get out to the lean-to I have a little cry. Not a real cry. Leaking tears and snivelling. There a petrol can and old-fashioned mop to fumble with. The mop hasn't been used in a while. If ever. What do you expect from a house run by a bunch of men?

There's a plastic bucket with a place to squeeze on one side. It's under the carpet that my footprints will register, even after the fire. I can use the petrol as a solvent to break up the sticky blood patches.

A deeper sorrow hollows my chest.

Ah, shit. Not now.

I wipe my eyes. Deep breaths. Keep it together. If I go back in and Dan sees me all red-eyed and sniffling it'll undo all my good work.

Fuuuuuck. Thiiiiis.

I should just kill him.

I really should.

I'm sure there are a hundred ways I could justify keeping him alive: I could use his cop computers to search for Bright-Eyes' license plate; he could become my secret ally in my fight against crime; I could climb on his dick and go bouncy. But really, I just want to prove that I'm not nearly as horrible as I've convinced myself I am. Saving dopey, deluded Dan will be my little bargain. That one nice thing we evil people do to convince ourselves we still have a shot at redemption.

There's a jerry can and another barely half full. I figured they'd have more, but maybe they weren't planning on being here that long. Headless seemed ready enough to snatch me up, from what my notes detail. I can't imagine them holding someone for more than a few days, a week at most. Maybe they didn't bother to re-stock, once the girl (that would be me) got away.

There's probably a heavenly conjunction they're trying to catch.

Ridiculous nonsense.

There was- Fuck! I'd give anything to just switch off my brain for half a second! Always thinking, thinking, thinking. Drive until I find a nice lay-by and snooze for a bit. Get myself together. Or just scream at the world for an hour or so.

I crouch, leaning on the mop for support, and look up, breathing. I have a lot to do tonight. If I'm keeping Dan alive, I'm going to make him work for it. He'll be the key to finding my prey.

I wipe the kitchen down, then drag Dan onto the stone floor, leaving the back door open, and him still securely tied. He keeps trying to engage me in conversation but I ignore him. Got work to do. I smudge the wall and manage to soak most of the areas where I seemed to have stood long enough, or landed with enough force, to make blood seep through to the rubber underlay. Then rub them over with the mop, just to be sure.

When I'm out of Dan's line of sight, I snag the wallet off the table. Pretty sure it's his. I'd like to go through the pockets of the rest of them for petrol money but I want Dan to have a higher opinion of me than that.

As I work, I wiggle my bum a bit for the detective's sake. I'm getting an itch down there and I've seen him looking. Contrary to popular belief, most men are shy. I'm hoping Dan's confident manner will translate to him having the confidence to make a pass at me, or at least, not reject me if I jump on him. He is cute. And I have the raging hormones of an eighteen year old. With luck, I'll have his pants off before the night's out.

The floor is flagstones under the carpet, so it won't burn and helpfully erase any trace evidence. There's an actual fireplace. I leave the flue wide open so the fire will draw. Open the front door, so it won't starve for want of oxygen. What little fuel remains, I spread over every surface then trickle a line back to the door. It's genuinely old, this place. The stone walls are plastered-over straw insulation. Should go up a treat. As will half the surrounding forest, which will down the discovery and investigation.

Oh! The vomit! I pour on enough to soak my DNA out of the chunder (it can be used as a noun as well as a verb).

I light the petrol, step back into the kitchen and stand over Dan, knife out. He looks at me with a feigned calmness as orange fire fills the room behind me, panic only revealed by the fact he has to breathe with his mouth open.

I think I've positioned him correctly.

Arms first, then, as he gets the feeling back, and some ideas into his head, I go down and cut the legs free, too. I rock back onto my haunches, deliberately crowding him. He stands, awkwardly, using the sink for support as he slides back, moving the chair aside, such that it blocks the doorway.

Perfect.

I casually kick the chair outside and sidle out. There's still tape on it. He follows, trying to think of something clever to do or say that will put him back in charge, where he's comfortable. I don't give him the chance.

"Now, Dan my man, you're going to have to carry me."

"Carry you? Why would I carry you?"

"Dan. The house is on fire. We don't have time for a discussion. This night was supposed to be a bit of covert intelligence gathering but saving your sorry arse has made the whole thing go tits-up for me. So, you're going to have to make amends for being alive." I can see the fight in his eyes. Also, I said tits and he flicked down for a look, so that's promising. "I'm sure, at some level, you're grateful that I. Saved. Your. Life. But right now, I need you to Do. As. You. Are. Told. Okay?" I'm not sure he heard. He doesn't even nod, so I just assume his compliance and continue giving orders. "Right. I can feel the heat starting to come off the house, so we have to be quick. I need you to pick me up and walk over all my foot prints out here, erase them as much as you can. My size nines are too easy to trace. In those boots, your steps will probably be mistaken for their footprints, much harder to distinguish."

Something crashes in the house behind.

I step up and place an arm around Dan's neck, the knife still in my other hand.

"Come on! Let's be quick about this!"

"Is that really..." He wants to speak, but the fire and my urgency are pushing him more than he can resist. "Okay. Fine." I'd like to think I don't weigh that much, but he doesn't seem to expend much effort lifting me. Strong.

Nice.

"I can't see." He's peering past me. "You haven't left any footprints. The ground's too hard. We haven't had rain all week."

"Yeah, I know. And it's coming up to summer, so drying out. Let's just do a quick stepping where I tell you. We'll spot the odd one here and there."

"Sure." He sighs. "Right"

Fucking attitude on him. We do a quick once over of the yard. I direct him around and through the woods, his chest heaving with effort against me, carefully retracing my steps. There's practically nothing. I'm just being paranoid but it's fun ordering him about, erasing, making new, random paths. I wriggle a little bit, just to keep him distracted, and because I'm enjoying writhing against his almost-manly chest.

"Oh, shit! Did you do that?" He asks, when we get up to the still and bloodied Watcher.

"You think someone else kicked his head in then slit his throat? No, don't put me down!" He puts me down. "Okay, fine. Have a rest. Yeah. I killed him. I also crouched behind him after, for a good while, checking out the scene. Make sure you step there."

"How the hell did you sneak up on him? These were soldiers. I mean, that's a C8 carbine, Special Forces issue, the new model. And those guys back in the cottage? There were three of them. Trained fighters. I mean, we were yelling a bit, but how did you take apart that many trained soldiers?"

"Actual Shaolin Masters, remember? Don't take that so lightly."

Lies, lies, lies. I'm sure Meng Laoshi, the nice old lady who teaches BaGuaZhang in the village hall every morning, would be tickled pink to hear herself described as a Shaolin Master. Dan looks around, impressed. If they don't see you fuck up, no need to tell them.

"Was he another friend of yours?" I ask, suspecting ulterior motives for the delay. "You knew him?"

"What? No. No, he wasn't part of my unit. He probably wasn't posted to the same place. It's usually a jumble, this sort of security job."

"Well, then stamp out my fucking footprints and let's go! Come on! We have to move, soldier."

Unfortunately, he's beginning to recover after his little trauma. Fuck, I hate it when clueless people start to get ideas. There's not enough time for me to patiently explain everything to someone who doesn't have much respect for anything I have to say.

Especially when Dan opens with, "Now, just hang on a minute-"

"Don't fucking start! There's a house on fire! Burning! Right there! We don't have a fucking minute, DAN. So let's do the twenty questions bit once we're the fuck out of here! Back that way." I point in the direction I entered. "And quickly!"

"Look I'm a police officer. I'm sure-"

"Stop thinking, Dan! This isn't about cops and robbers, calming the witnesses, explaining things to your boss, who I'm sure is a lovely and understanding person. This is about a gang of military-trained killers fucking hunting us down. We want to give them as little as possible. I promise we can do the whole, 'Who should be in charge' thing once we get back to the fucking car. Now, pick me the fuck up!"

This is going to be a nightmare.

We make it back over the hill with an angry-but-silent Dan thinking dangerously all the way. To give him credit, he's diligent about stepping over my footprints, if we see any.

I can't have him carry me the whole way back to the car, he's getting tired and it's just impractical. Forensics will focus on the cottage, but they may walk the edges, if they can track Dan's footprints at all. Fortunately, my jump into the woods has left a possibility.

"Okay, Dan. How are you doing?" I ask as we descend the hill.

"Fine," he answers. "You're not that heavy. I can manage."

"That's not exactly what I meant, but sure. We only need to get to the edge of the woods, just down there, and then you can put me down. Well, a little bit past."

He steps on, silent. O! This is going wrong in every way. I can tell already. Sulky, sooky bastard. Heroes in stories always have a companion, mostly so they can explain themselves and remind everyone how cool they are.

I can't have company.

No sidekick, no little Scooby gang. It just doesn't work like that for me. People always want to know exactly what's going on, all the details that I don't even understand myself. I mean, I'm over seventy and I still look eighteen.

How the fuck does that work?

This bloody knee of mine has been giving me shit for fifty years. It's definitely better than it was, so is it healing?

What the fuck is happening with me?

My fingernails break at the slightest pretext but I can punch a hole in someone's face and not bruise my knuckles. I don't get my period, but I can cry, nay weep, if the mood strikes me.

I have trouble making new memories, even remembering what day it is. The ditzy artist persona helps so much with that. Once I write it all down, it seems to stick. I write it longhand, because I read somewhere that helps with memory and neuro-function thingies. Can you imagine if someone actually found one of my stories and typed it up? Nightmare. I mean, I write as if I'm explaining things to a room full of people. Like I'm back at my very preppy school, on stage with the theatre club and this is all one big monologue to my future self. Plus, I can change bits as I'm writing it to have a better image of myself, or take the edge off things that are super painful.

How do I explain my crazy thing to someone else? It's too crazy for me to understand. Anyone else have that problem? Are you so secretly insane you have to act super-normal?

If I have the detective along for any length of time, I'm going to have to make up a whole new bunch of lies, and that'll get confusing for you as well as me. I think Puppy is the only one who even has an inkling, but she's wise enough not to ask questions. Fuck it. Let's get out of this fucking forest.

We break out of the tree-line and I immediately feel exposed, clumping down to the edge of the field. The night is bright, the hedges low, recently trimmed. The mottled dimness of English countryside sweeps majestically in all directions, not a light to be seen.

"Okay. Stop here," I tell Dan. "Keep one foot back, like you're mid-stride. We're going to create a little narrative for the forensic team. If they even get this far. That's it. Good." He stops where I said, how I said. Thank fuck he's good at taking orders. "Great. Now. I'm going to slide down and stand on your feet. It won't hurt if you're ready for it."

"I'm ready. It's fine."

Still sulking? Huh, whatever. I ease down, grinding deliberately along him, especially the hips. Is that his dick, or just his keys? I can't tell. I haven't woken him all the way. Professionalism usually has its limits. He's not gay. I've seen him looking. And he tracked across two counties to chat me up. We'll have time for that later, with any luck.

I brace on his front foot, swing my other leg forward and launch after it, twisting in mid-air to land in the same directions as my previous footprints. I didn't worry too much about leaving any. I thought this was going to be a sneaky operation. Bloodless. I really should know better by now.

Dan has a slightly impressed face. Well, that was a good three metres. Too much?

"Now," I tell him, "you'll have to chase me."

"What?"

I scrabble about, blurring my footprints in an approximation of panic, then set off at a good pace.

"Hey!" he calls. Loud. Stupid. "Just hold it right there!"

Oh, fuck me. All the cliché lines.

"Will you stop yelling, moron!" I hiss, loud as I dare. "Now, keep up! Come on!"

I turn and run, stumbling about in 'hysteria', and frankly not giving a damn if the walking stereotype is keeping up or not. He has a personality under there somewhere. I've seen glimpses. Maybe he's just freaked out by the whole evening's proceedings.

We make it to the road, and I leap the gate, mostly because I'm enjoying the run, and flying through the air in the dark of night makes me feel like Batman. I pull it back, so it just looks like a good jump. I know, I know. I should say it makes me feel like Batwoman.

When I turn, Dan is right behind me. He vaults the gate. Kind of impressive. Landing, he seems anxious, panting, like he's trying to work out which direction I'm going to bolt.

It always amazes me how people with an obvious degree of intelligence can be so fucking clueless sometimes.

Huh. Like I'm perfect.

"Okay. Car's this way," I tell him. "Down the lane, just there."

"Car? What? What the hell was that for?"

At least he's whispering.

"It's a narrative. The footprints make it look like you came out of the woods, surprised a woman, chased her." I'm trying to stop my shoulders hunching in frustration. "Unless you'd rather carry me the whole fucking way down here."

"Right. Right. Fine. Whatever."

He's shaking his head, lost, confused and out of breath. Dan is not handling his lack of control very well.

Maybe that's his thing. Knowing everything all the time. He did sort of mention that at the cottage, when talking about knowing what he was doing, investigating the righteousness of it all. Or maybe he's used to being in control. Either way, he's going to have a hard time with me.

"Come on. Car. What? Did you think I walked here from fucking Elstead? Come on." I reach out. "You can hold my hand if you like. Might make it more natural looking if someone spots us."

Dan glances at my hand, ignores it (damn), and furrows his brow. "Where the hell are we?"

"Back side of the hill from the cottage. I'm not stupid enough to drive up to the front door."

"No, I mean, where the hell are we? I was brought here in the back of a van."

"Oh, right. We're in the Chilterns."

"The Chilterns? That's a pretty wide area to cover."

"Yeah. There're a couple of little villages scattered about, but nothing within a mile or so. I'll show you on the GPS, once we're back at the car. I think these nouveau-riche mansions are the closest buildings; the rest of the village is farther on. Which is handy for a training house."

"Training house? That's where they train the girls? Oh, shit. Those beds."

"Yes. Those beds, with the iron rings bolted onto the frames scratched by handcuffs, musty sheets that aren't cleaned regularly, woodwork scuffed from struggles where they hold the girls down and gang rape them, over and over and over. Fun times."

"Shit." He looks genuinely upset. Actual feelings. Wow. "I had no idea I was getting... I just..."

Oh, it's the guilt thing! That's what's fucking him up! Let's see if we can't get him to open up long enough for me to pull the rest of that stick out of his arse. "Did you actually believe your friends when they got in touch with you? Or have you done stuff like this for them before?"

He glances at me in the night, features blurred by dimness but still distinct enough to register his shame. "I... This, er... This wasn't the first time. I've checked a couple of criminal files and stuff, but they're private security. Registered. Certified. They can run their own licence plate searches, background checks. This is the first time I ran fingerprints for them. The results came back really quickly, too. That made me kind of suspicious, made me want to have a chat with you about your mother. Or, you, I suppose. Those are your fingerprints we have on file, aren't they?"

"Yeah. As you said, luck always runs out. I got careless and left a nice left-hand set on a window I forgot I opened. A couple of partials from the right hand ended up at some other scene, I never found out how."

"You've been doing this for how long?"

"I don't 'Do This'. Not the way you mean. I suppose since I was seventeen, so, well, you can do the math. But I don't, 'Do This' as a thing. Not like my mother did. I know there are a couple of attributions in my file that have nothing to do with me."

More lies. I know there are several I've done that haven't been attributed to me. This all started a few years after I emerged from my red pit of hell. Three months before my nineteenth birthday they took me to that domed room under the earth and birthed me. But that was so long ago. It took me years to mature, discover some purpose for my life. Then I had to die and be reborn as my own daughter.

This is confusing for you, isn't it? Two dates for everything. Two different people. When I'm talking about my mother, I'm actually talking about me, most of the time. Plus, you have to remember that half of what I say to Dan is a lie. I tell you the truth. Mostly.

Confusing.

Fuck, I wish I could tell someone everything, just be totally honest and not judged. Wishful thinking. It's that whole, 'not being judged' part that fucks me every time. Even you're judging me, reading this coated-in-so-much-sugar-you'll-vomit version.

Nobody is really this smart, sassy with their dialogue, internal or otherwise.

You don't know what I'm really like.

It's so hard to stay sane and focussed and not allow a moment of loneliness, weakness, to creep in. Perhaps that's the real reason I'm keeping the nice detective with the nice hair alive. He seems smart enough to understand. Maybe.

In my fucking dreams.

"Quiet now," I say to him. "There are houses."

We slip down the lane towards the imposing walls of someone else's idea of a country seat. Dan wanders past me, not too close, peering cautiously through the iron-stalked gate at the dark windows.

"Careful," I tell him. "Motion sensors."

He glances about and eases back. I unlock the rear and fish out my spare clothes from the small suitcase, neatly rolled in a heavy-duty garbage bag, dumping them on the floor of the boot. Trackie daks, a long-sleeve tee, canvas shoes and a fleece vest, all in darker, neutral colours. All from charity bins.

Oh, 'daks' is Australian slang for trousers, so tracksuit bottoms, or sweatpants, are called Trackie Daks. I like the way it sounds.

I unzip my camo-jacket and deliberately inside-out it as I take it off, tucking the blood-sprayed mess into the tough, plastic bag. This whole '5p for a bag' thing gives me an excuse to use garbage bags, because shopping bags are getting so difficult to find.

When I pull off my top, Dan snorts and says, "Are you trying to shock me, or something?"

"I don't know, Dan." I pop the button on my cargo pants and open the zip. A little shimmy and they start to drop. "How easily shocked, are you?"

He gives me a quick appraisal. I don't want to boast. No, seriously, please don't stop liking me. Look, I hate my body as much as the next person. But let's face it, I did ballet growing up. Trained to be a professional. Trained hard for years. I was on the hockey team in college, trained regularly. My mum was a war-rationed, anti-hippy. Until she married my dad. She was very strict about sweets and followed every fad diet for children that ever emerged. And I'm not short. My boobs came in a little on the small side, but with the right pose, they look okay. Not in this sports bra, though.

I have the body of a fit eighteen year old. From the '60s or '70s, before this idea of being ridiculously skinny took hold. Well, I suppose there was Twiggy.

Oh shit. My bandaid!! I glance down, but no, it's fine. The hand-long medical dressing under my ribs is still firmly attached in spite of all the excitement.

That's not what the detective is looking at, in any case. Dan opens his mouth to say something, then shakes his head and turns away.

Ha! I made him go non-verbal! Love it when I do that.

I sit on the tail of the car to pull my boots off and get out of my cargo pants, stuffing it all into the leak-proof sack. Always use the good garbage bags when you're committing crime, not the cheapo, thin ones. Seriously.

I slip the bra off for a moment and fluff the girls a little, shuffle about making random noises to pass the time, then strike a pose, sucking my tummy in just enough, hands on hips, prominent chest.

"It's okay. I'm dressed."

Dan turns and sees me even more naked than before and, "Oh, Jeez!" Turns away.

I have trouble not laughing very, very loudly.

"Oh, that was totally worth it!" I whisper. "The look on your face! Priceless."

"That was completely unnecessary!" he whispers, mock-shocked, but chuckling along with the joke, and actually embarrassed at his own embarrassment. Dan, you are so not the cool guy. Even in that shirt.

Actually, we really need to do something about that shirt, his whole ensemble is a tad, shall we say, smeared-in-blood. And the smeared look is not in this year. I pull out my wet-towel, rub down thoroughly. It's all through my hair and, fuck, I need a shower. And so does he.

The possibilities.

I dress quickly.

For the moment, I unroll another couple of garbage bags, sliding one over the seat back and puffing the other out to cover the seat itself. Dan works out that I'm properly dressed and comes over to help. He gets in the way, so I shoo him off. There. That should catch the worst of the drips.

Antonio will do a thorough cleaning inside and out when I dump the car with him. Or maybe I should use the garage down in Winchester? University kids are always on the lookout for a cheap, reliable car, and they'll be far less fussy about random stains.

Dan has appointed himself watchman and lookout, mostly so he doesn't have to look at me.

"Okay, Detective," I whisper.

Dan turns, a slender figure in the night.

"Right. So. Now what?"

"Now," I tell him, "you're going to help me break into the local police headquarters."

"And why the hell would I do that?"

"Because, Detective Dan, you left your fingerprints all over that crime scene. I wiped mine down, but yours are on the ceramic sink, on that metal chair I kicked outside, and your DNA lurks in the folds of duct tape I left all over the back garden. Do you have any idea how much forensic evidence they can gather from the scene of a fire?"

# 9

# Headquarters

Aylesbury's a fucked-up town. If anywhere can be said to perfectly capture the schizo nature of modern Britain, this comes pretty fucking close.

Right next door is the amazing Waddesdon Manor where Queen Victoria once came to stay. The gorgeous Wendover Woods, with well-defined pathways, children's play areas and, of course, lots of trees. In town, there is a well-preserved fifteenth century pub, buried behind some '40s town-houses turned into shops.

Which gives us a hint as to what is very, very wrong.

Way too much dead-red-brick.

Also incongruous, modern buildings jammed together with no plan or rhythm, swamping what little original architecture remains. The town centre is a shit-hole. It also contains the hideous building that houses the Headquarters for Buckinghamshire Police. A huge block of red brick in a sea of shitty red brick. Literally, just a block.

This is '70s architecture at it's worst.

There are other square blocks jammed up against it, with a lot of nasty wire fencing. It certainly serves to amply represent the bastion of male authority that it contains. I mean, I'm sure it didn't even look good in the architect's drawing. But they built it anyway. It's as messy as a student house populated entirely by boys. The debris from the nearby trees, grime from the city, years of poorly cleaned windows, the stagnant pond. No, seriously. That could well be in the running for the ugliest pond in England.

Let's just say I'm thankful I'm only seeing it at night.

And in typical police fashion, the buzzer on the back gate doesn't work properly. Dan is still sulking from his foolishness at the cottage. He wants to get out, run around and enter the manual code, but that'll look too suspicious on the cameras. He reluctantly tells it to me. I lean out with my hood up and knuckle it in. I won't tell you what it is.

"Where are the other cameras?" I enquire.

"Oh, apart from the one at the gate, the only one back here is on the door. Doesn't cover the far side of the carpark at all."

"And the one on the far corner, that's... What? Checking no one is going to climb over the fence?"

"Huh? Oh, yeah. Well spotted. Forgot about that one. It's mostly used to catch people pissing up against the tree. Or the wall. There's always someone who thinks that's... I don't know. Rebellious."

"And you never rebelled?"

"Never really had anything to rebel against. Maybe I was rebelling against rebellion."

I huff my amusement. Men like it when you laugh at their jokes. Especially the lame ones. And I *really* want him to like me. A lot. Did I mention I was itchy down there?

"Who's on the back door?" I ask. "Do you know them?"

"Oh, it's not manned after nine." It's long after nine. "There are no holding cells here, so the front security desk monitors all the cameras at night. This is mostly admin, residential liaison. I don't actually work here."

"You don't even work here?"

"No, I work out of the station at-"

"But you have a locker here?"

"Well, no, but I know where they are. We do courses here. There's a gym downstairs. Showers. Toilets. Male and female. You said we should shower. Clean all this crap off. And there are lockers. You said you were good with locks. We can get some spare clothes for me from one of them." He indicates the mess on his shirt. "Look, you're the one who wanted to come here!"

"Fine, fine. We'll wing it. No problem."

Now the fear starts eating my insides. This is going to be way more dangerous than I thought. Normally, I research things. Google maps, blueprints, electrical wiring grid to help locate the cameras. Shit. I hate this seat-of-the-pants stuff. Perhaps that's adding to my excitement. My pulse is definitely rising. I think that's because of something else I want to do with Dan.

Pulling around to park where I'm told, I notice Dan is getting used to being in charge again. It's a dangerous line to play with. I'll have to see how he responds when I yank his chain.

Okay. We exit the vehicle and proceed in an orderly manner up to the back door. Detective Dan enters a code on the metal keypad and (*buzz*) the door opens. I have the hood up on my fleece, picking something out of my teeth to distort any glimpse the cameras get of my face, and we're inside.

"Right. Changing rooms are down this way."

Dan leads off and I follow, fussing with my hair to keep a hand in front of my face, in case we meet anyone. The place feels weird, like most offices at night. There should be people here, bustling, chatting, working.

Dan seems surprisingly unconcerned about bumping into a random officer in his blood-soaked shirt. It's like he's some sort of policeman himself. Oh, wait. He is.

There are concrete stairs down to a concrete basement. I get the feeling concrete might well be an architectural theme. "Okay. This is the gents. The ladies is just down there, on the left."

"Yeah. This isn't a cheesy horror movie. We're not splitting up."

"I... Look. That's..."

"Don't be such a prude, Dan. Come on. We haven't got all night. You'll just have to try and contain yourself."

Like I'm going to contain myself. Doing it in the locker-room of a police station? Oh, I'm such a naughty girl. He doesn't know what he's in for. I'm going to get my fingers into that nice hair. Oh, yes. But we really should get clean before we get dirty.

There are rows of grey, metal lockers, wooden benches with hooks above them, a couple of uniform jackets left out. The latches on the locker doors are a joke. I don't even need my tools, just this little trick I learned for dial padlocks. I won't tell you what it is. We find a few clothes left behind, or ready for the next day.

First, he needs to get out of those dirty things.

The showers are farther in, a strip of nozzles in a big, tiled space. You know the kind of thing. The tiles are an ugly, bright white-with-orange-flecks. I'm not concerned with the tiles.

Dan tries his best to be professional, discreetly turning his back as he strips.

Poor boy.

We do wash.

There are soap dispensers on the wall and everything.

Body-wise, he's not a muscle man, but he is fit. There's the hint of a six-pack, muscles moving as he cleans. He's looking. Stealing glimpses of me.

He tries to be casual about it and asks, "What's with the, er, bandage thing."

There's steam around us.

I glance down at the strip underneath one breast and decide to tell him a half-truth. "It's from a knife wound."

He seems unconvinced. "Did a pot break and you scratched yourself on it?"

"You're quite the detective, Detective. Now kneel down a minute. You've got some stuff on the back of your head I need to wash off."

Time for some hair porn. I rub suds into his thick locks, ostensibly cleaning things. His head moves as I curl and massage his delicious mane, then I snake my way around to the front. He lasts about two seconds with my boobs in his face before I comment, "Funny. You're kneeling and standing to attention at the same time."

He glances away, tries to get up, but I take hold of his arm, and he's surprised by my strength.

"Dan, Dan, Dan. Being the nice guy is all well and good, but there's a point where even that becomes rude." I cradle his head in my hands as he kneels naked before naked me. "A true gentleman would never refuse a polite and reasonable request from a lady." I lift one leg and run my foot slowly up his thigh, breath coming faster, exposing myself completely. "Now, I might be a long fucking way away from being a lady, but I am asking you, very politely, to take your cock and shove it right up my cunt. Pretty fucking please with a cherry on top." I press my foot against his manhood as I say that. It twitches against my toes. And men wonder why girls giggle. "Can you manage that for me?"

There's a catch in his breath. "I, um. I don't really know what to say."

I curl over and move my face next to his, my breath on his lips, "Say, yes ma'am."

"...yes ma'am."

We kiss, and it's awkward, too hesitant and too hard, and this is hardly the best position, but I can work with that. I give him a couple of little hints, about how to work my breasts. Long and gentle strokes at first. "You can squeeze them a bit harder later, but not too hard."

We kiss and writhe for a while, and I caress his nice cock. He gets a few direct instructions when he's got his fingers up inside me. "Curl them a little, just hold there and let me move."

His confidence comes back, lifting me off the ground and sucking my nipples, and it's really amazing. Not too hard. He remembered not too hard.

Oh, you have no idea. No, seriously, you don't. I'm sure you've fucked, or not, or whatever, but it's not just extreme pain that causes a feed-back of sensation from the sun, swimming with my daemon in an ecstasy like nothing "OH FUCK!" like nothing on this Earth.

I have to hold myself in check, so I don't lose control and rip him apart.

Oh, wow, my hips are taking over, grinding against him. He's wiggling his fingers in there beautifully, then starts moving his whole body up and down in long strokes against mine. Damn, Soldier! That's some good work!

I move us out of the shower stream so the water doesn't wash away all the lubrication I've spent the last hour building up. I have a little orgasm when bends down to lick my belly in gentle circles, still working those fingers. When he gets inside, I climb right up him like he's a sweaty, sexy tree.

I like someone I can climb.

We grind there for a while until his arms get tired, so I hop down and turn around. He seems a bit surprised when I bend over and hold onto the show taps.

I have to keep control. Just a little bit of control.

He grabs my hips with a bit of urgency and gets all up in that thing, gives me some of that good, hard fucking from behind. It doesn't take him long to finish.

So much for professionalism.

Dammit, if he isn't all ashamed of himself afterwards. He gets his panting under control, looking nervously about, can't meet my eyes. My knees are shaky, and I'm fighting back a fit of the giggles. I always get that after.

I didn't hear anyone come in, but I might have missed it in all the excitement. I take a couple of damp steps and poke my head out. Nah, no one there.

He turns his back and starts washing himself down again.

I place a hand on his back and he actually flinches.

"Just don't."

"Oh, come on, Dan. Do you have a girlfriend, or something? I'm guessing no, from the way you've been eyeing me up all evening. Come on. Doesn't matter. Two naked people as pretty as us in a shower together, what did you think was going to happen?"

"We just- No, I don't have, er, that was- You tricked me into this whole thing."

"Tricked you?" No girlfriend. So, what the hell's the matter with him? "I seduced you. That's very different."

"It's the same thing."

"No, it's not. I didn't make you do anything you didn't already want to do."

"Well, we shouldn't have done that."

"Yes! We should have done that!" I rub his back. "Trust me on this. Life is short. Youth is fleeting." Well, for some. "We definitely should have done that."

He huffs and wanders out in search of a towel. I linger, sighing in the stream, and give myself a little special attention as my knees settle. I find the smell does tend to linger for me if I don't scrape out as much as I can. Does anyone else have that? It's not a bad smell, and maybe it's only me that notices it. I like to clean myself out a bit. Probably it's just a habit.

Then the door to the locker room opens.

"Inspector!" says Dan.

Oh, fuck my life.

"Oh, it's, er, Daniel, isn't it? I remember you from the computer competency course, couple of weeks back, isn't that it?" He sounds old. Shit. Just what I need. Some stuffy old fart whose body I'm going to have to hide.

"Oh, yes sir. That'll be it. Detective Sergeant Ripplewater."

"Ha! Knew you even with your shirt off! Don't mind me. I'm just having a crap before I pop upstairs. Got some files to drop off." Footsteps shuffle. Other sounds echo off the tiles: squeaking, clattering, the tinkling of a loosened belt buckle.

I poke my head out from the showers and can only see a closed toilet door. Presumably, the person on the loo can't see out but I don't want to make extra shadows on the tiled floor.

"So, what brings you to our neck of the woods then, lad? This time of night?"

Oh, fuck. He's actually going to have a conversation while he's shitting. Do guys do that? Well, this guy certainly does.

"Oh, er, I'm on night shift. It's quiet at the station and there's this missing person's case, sir." Dan sees me and tosses me a spare towel, gesticulating incomprehensibly. "Threw up an unusual file. Might be a foreign connection. I wanted to try and get access to some of the European databases, the CCF at Interpol, maybe the SIS, see what I could dig out. Thought I'd make a quick visit to the gym before getting to work. Bit out of breath."

"Huh! Bloody Shengen nonsense," comes the hollow, echoing voice from the cubicle. "I can't see why we didn't join up straight away."

This is like a French farce. Fucking awesome! I pat myself down so my footsteps won't squelch. Sticking to the wall, I carefully slip over and lift my clothes off the bench.

"Too damned useful not to be a part of it, especially if we're going to open the bloody floodgates, like we have."

Slipping back into the showers, I pick a corner and begin a quick, but thorough drying.

"Bloody politics for you. Well, you're in, oof. You're in luck."

Oh my fucking god, I just heard the splash of a police inspector letting one drop!

"I can't help you with Interpol, you'll have to put in a request for that, but I can get you a login, ahhhh, for the SIS. Just one of those temporary thingies."

I'm killing myself trying not to laugh. It's seriously interfering with me getting dressed quickly.

"Yeah. They mentioned those on the course." Dan sounds strange. "That's actually exactly what I was hoping to get from the night-duty officer."

"Oh, no need to bother old Sammy with that. I'm sure he wouldn't even know what one is. Now. Hang about for two seconds, I'll walk you up there."

"Thank you, sir. I'll, er, just see if my colleague is waiting outside." I point at the showers and rotate my hands. "Oh, I'll just turn the showers off, first."

Like he had to narrate that.

Dan wanders over, wide eyed and making faces, trying to communicate something. I'm too busy not laughing to give a fuck what he's trying to say.

Dan has on a pair of pants and a boring, white shirt that fits him. I prefer the interesting-coloured ones. Oh, crap, what are we going to do with his bloodied clothes on the bench? I brought a folded-up garbage bag in my pocket, but if the inspector is going to walk us up the stairs... Fuck. I'll have to think of something.

I manage to flick the showers off without getting soaked, then gesture to Dan that he should head for door. I follow, matching him step-for-step to mask my own footfalls. One shadow.

The toilet seat clatters as the inspector rises, done with his business. There's a bit of shuffling about and I panic jump to the door, deliberately banging it open.

"Hah! Caught ya! Ah, ya dressed. Damn. I was too slow!" The inspector emerges, an amused look on his rough old face. "Oh! Inspector!" I pretend to be surprised. "So sorry, I didn't realise you were in here. I was just- Sorry. I'll wait out-"

"That's all right, lass, we're all decent."

"Well, I don't know about decent, sir, but..."

Everyone chuckles at my joke. Even Dan. He's actually not bad at this subterfuge stuff. He doesn't force the laugh. Maybe it's his Special Forces training. Or did he think it was funny?

"And you are?"

"Oh. Er. Tracy, sir." I try to act embarrassed instead of guilty. There's a fine line. "Detective Constable-" Shit, what would be a good last name? Bent-over-in-the-shower-and-loving-it? Bent-over- "Tracy Wendover, sir. Dan and I were just using the gym. We've got this missing person's case, and a lot of downtime on the night-shift."

"Yes, yes. Daniel was just telling me about it. You wanted to get some computer time."

"Yes, sir. That's right. Dan's just done a course here and mentioned something about a temporary login?"

I'm not sure how well the nice old man can see my face without his glasses. He recognised Dan well enough. I have my hood up and I'm fussing nervously with hair I didn't have time to brush, head dipped slightly in embarrassment.

"Yes, yes. Should be fine. As I said, Daniel has already filled me in."

The inspector has a nice line in benevolent-old-man faces and doesn't seem to blink at the idea that I'm a woman, or that I came crashing into the men's lockers. I was fully expecting him to launch into a stuffy-old-sexist tirade, then I could get a bit shirty before going all apologetic. My usual thing. This relaxed attitude of his has thrown me completely.

"Did you want to run your stuff back to the car?" Dan asks, making me confused until I cotton on. "We'll be up on the third floor."

"Yeah, I'll just go grab it. You two go ahead, I'll be up in a tick."

I stroll down towards the women's locker room. That was sharp. Damn, but I do like the smart ones. Dan is showing great promise, manoeuvring me out of the way so Inspector Let's Not Remember His Name doesn't get a decent look at me, securing a login, then heading up... Just him and... Suddenly my stomach goes cold.

Dan's going to betray me!

The fucker!

He's got himself alone with the inspector and sent me off so he can dump me in it! Except there is a very bloody shirt in thelocker room. DNA all over it.

Shit.

Did I just fall for a simple play, or did he just seriously raise my opinion of him? I've never killed a police inspector, before. Or an entire station worth of cops. Or whatever skeleton crew is left to man this place at night. All the concrete will make it difficult to burn.

Oh, this is bad.

Or good.

My legs can't decide. By the time I reach the locker-room door, my knees are weak and wobbly again. I have to grab onto the handle just for support. Half-swimming from our session, I'm still all tingly. It's been a while, and damn but that was just what I needed.

Except now I can't keep it together and I'm going to get us both in trouble, hands uncertain, brain like lead hitting clay, heavy and unmanageable. Physical pain sets me swimming but this emotional torment I have to endure in full. The daemon likes to watch me suffer.

Fucker.

A casual look back shows Dan and the inspector climbing the stairs, chatting quietly. What's he saying? Why can't I have, like, super-hearing and x-ray vision to go along with the rest of it?

Fuck!

Once the two of them are climbing the second flight, I sprint back along the corridor and dart into the men's lockers, already pulling the garbage bag from my pocket. Moving is good. Just keep moving. Deal with each crisis as it comes. I collect all of the evidence. A sick little part of me wants to smell his clothing and see if the scent of Dan has lingered, but there's also a lot of blood-scent, and I can't let myself get attached. No.

It's bad enough that I named him.

Into the bag with all of it, wrapped and tied tight.

Even if he proves to be super helpful, he'll never understand. Just like the rest of them. No point in trying.

I head up and out, feeling far too conspicuous by myself. What the fuck do I do if I meet anyone? I don't have a badge. Where the hell has Dan really gone? I hate this shit. But then, what the fuck did I think was going to happen when I wandered into a police station all unprepared?

In the dank carpark, I dump the bag in the Corolla with the rest of the forensic wet-dream of evidence, and my incriminatingly lined handbag, then head back inside.

I can recall the code for the back door because I traced it onto my palm when Dan punched it in. It's a neat little trick to help me remember things. I did some research on different types of amnesia when I worked out that was part of my problem. I used the same trick for Bright-Eyes' number plate when he and Dan visited my cottage.

As I'm climbing the stairs I can't help but think, *What am I walking into, here?*

At the landing, I'm just in time to see the inspector hand DS Ripplewater something that looks like a business card. That might be the login.

I fade back into the stairwell, peeping around, spying out any further interactions that might give away if Dan's got a plan. Inspector No-Name provides some minor instructions, going over protocols and such. Then he pats Dan on the back, picks up a small bag, and heads in my direction. Going home for the evening? Well, it is after midnight.

"Heading home for the evening, sir?" I enquire as I emerge casually from the stairwell.

"Yes, thank you, er-"

"Tracy, sir."

"Tracy! Yes. Of course. Wendover. As much as I enjoy cluttering up these offices with my useless old bones, I do still have to sleep."

"Yeah, my dad was the same. Always a bit of night owl, but really liked his sleep, especially after he retired."

"Your father can't be that old, surely?"

"Oh, he married late, retired early. Did Dan get the code thingy?"

"Oh, yes. Yes, I gave him the login, a brief reminder of the protocols."

"Thank you, sir. It's very kind of you. I won't forget it."

"Oh, don't mention it." The old man's chest broadens with pride. "We're here to help, after all. It's a constant source of frustration how many of my fellow officers forget that. As police officers, we're supposed to be helping people, not just ourselves or our careers."

"Huh. Yeah. I'll try and keep that in mind, sir. Thank you. Er. Night, then."

The inspector smiles benevolently. "Good night, Tracy."

He did tell me his name. I'm not going to mention it, just in case. He's a nice old man. Well, he's nice to me, but then I'm young and white and he thinks I'm a little piggy like him.

If he's an inspector, he's either well aware of the corruption and shittiness or good enough at being oblivious to it all so as to rise through the ranks. After all, this is the fucking Chilterns, not some den of vice and temptations.

And it looks like Dan has come up a notch.

I find my straight man in the far corner of a room full of computers and no-one else, his mop of hair poking up from behind a partition. I want to mash it all down and see how funny a shape I can make out of his face. Ha. Things are going too well, but then, I know what's going to happen next, so I guess that's fair.

"Got us a link yet?" I ask as I saunter over.

He makes a few slightly suspicious clicks with the mouse but cheerfully confirms, "Yeah. We're in."

"Awesome. For a second, I thought you were going to turn me in."

I thought that for a lot longer than a second.

"Well..." He leans back all smug looking. "I was tempted but then I remembered I couldn't find any other shoes, and these boots," he pulls out one foot and wiggles it at me, "still have traces of blood on them."

"Huh. Plus the shirt."

"It is a very distinctive shirt."

"Nothing wrong with that," I say. "I like those shirts you wear."

"Yeah, my sister picks them out for me. She has a good eye."

"Huh." Somehow, that's more disappointing than it should be. "Still," I say, grabbing a chair and wheeling it over. "You did okay with all the pretending stuff."

"Yeah. I did enjoy that. We get this Intel and Interaction course in the army, but posted to the Middle East, someone like me never got a chance to apply it."

"What? You never had to extract information from an informant? No thumbscrews and whips?"

"That's not what I meant. And no. Not my department, though we did escort a couple over from the American base once the Yanks had their information protocols amended."

"You mean, when they weren't allowed to torture people any more."

Dan seems slightly offended. "And how do you get your information exactly?"

I peer at him sidelong as I sit and pull myself closer. "Not through torture. Torture doesn't work. That's one of my problems. I find these people and I have to get to the next step by careful cross-referencing of several sources. If I could just hurt one of them until they tell me things, my life would be a lot simpler. People will yell anything when in pain. I always have to check. Always confirm."

He chuckles. "Absolutely. I expected nothing less."

"No, seriously. If you start hurting people, they're not going to be helpful. They will instantly hate you and want to lie. You have to break them completely, and that takes time, or such an extreme amount of physical abuse they're likely to die before they tell you anything. Even then, the fuckers still lie. You have to cross-reference. You're a cop. You know this. The police don't bother with that whole sweating the witness thing any-more. What is it you call it now? PEACE? Preparation. Engage. All that?"

"Well, that's a useful framework. Each interviewer develops their own individual style. I have a habit of interrupting the Account when the subject is giving their version of events, because they'll wander off topic or get things wrong." He chuckles again. "You must be an expert, sending me completely off track like you did."

"They're always expecting my mum, and I just tell you I'm not my mum, and that's true."

"Ha! Yes. That is true."

"Glad you're having fun."

"Maybe it's just my rebellious streak finally coming out. Or maybe I just didn't feel like betraying anyone today."

"This isn't rebellion, Dan. This is self-preservation. You're stuck in this too deeply. Life in danger and all that. And you are betraying someone. In fact, you're betraying the entire United Kingdom police force, you vile betrayer."

"Right. Exactly what am I getting myself into?"

"Oh, nothing too serious. Not getting cold feet, are we?"

"No, no. I'm in. Mostly because the inspector reminded me that as a police officer-"

"You're supposed to be helping people?"

Dan actually laughs at that. "Yeah! I think he only has the one speech." And there's that quirkiness that makes me want to smell his shirt and- OKAY!

Focus.

Dan indicates the computer. "So, what is it you want me to do?"

"I want you to get right the fuck out of my way while I call the Moroccan."

# 10

## Bed

"Why must I always work with people who are dimmer than a black hole and twice as dense? You should apologise to every tree that is working to replace the oxygen you waste by your miserable existence!"

I have to suppress a smile, too buzzed after my good ol' time in the shower to let Basila even remotely get to me.

"Yeah, no. I've plugged my phone in, Bas."

"Finally! Wonderful. Now, get yourself back to that command prompt. And hold that damned camera steady, man."

Dan doesn't take well to criticism, but is more bemused by Basila's nature.

"I'm getting some books and stuff to prop it up, okay?" he consoles.

Trying to hack a computer system while someone on Telegraph is giving you instructions based on what they can see of your screen from your boyfriend's phone is no easy task, let me tell you. Especially when your cameraman doesn't have steady hands.

Dan finishes his little Rube Goldberg construction of unopened post-it notes, rubber bands, and protocol manuals. "There. How's that?"

"It's the wrong angle, man," Basila complains. "Sister, why must we put up with this zemel?"

"I can assure you, sister, he's not a zemel," I reply, chuckling to myself. "Let me tilt the screen down a bit and then wedge this envelop under the phone…"

"What's a zememel?" Dan asks.

"Zemel. Means faggot," I tell him. "There. Is that better?"

"A thousand times!" comes Basila's jubilant response. "Now, type what I tell you." She begins listing of a string of commands. I do my best to keep up.

"You know, some of my best friends are faggots," Dan informs me.

"Really?"

"Yeah. Sam and Tanvir. Nice couple."

"Why is the man interrupting?" Basila asks.

"Says he has friends who are zemel. I'm not sure if that means he's offended or not."

"Well, tell him to takool zeb ala hamada. I'm trying to concentrate. Delete that last command and type this instead."

"What did she say?" asks Dan loudly.

I think he's winding Basila up on purpose after she refused to apologise for calling him an absurd, over-privileged, white-male infidel. Then immediately said, "And you can call me Bas, everyone here does, even if they're too ludicrously foolish to realise it doesn't mean anything."

Basila is a bit of an acquired taste. She's the most deliberately offensive person I've ever met, but she has a great sense of humour. I've always been of the opinion that the insults help her concentrate.

"She told you to eat the dick of a donkey," I translate.

"Well, I'm not going to do that, Bas. Not because I'm rejecting your suggestion, but mainly because this is Buckinghamshire, so I have no idea where to even find a donkey. Petting zoo, maybe? I don't know."

Now I'm laughing so hard I forget what I typed and have to go back while Basila curses me for fucking with male whores instead of concentrating.

A quick glance about and still no-one. A few people have gone past on the other side of the frosted security glass. We've heard movement, speaking on other floors, but no-one has come in, no-one has bothered us. I've barely seen another police officer since I came in here. Granted, most of them are downstairs doing whatever it is policemen do on a Tuesday after midnight. I thought the joint would be a bit livelier than this.

The local police stations deal with the night-shifts, crimes, and reports. Crimes are not reported here, so there aren't many actual police in this headquarters. I suppose Scotland Yard has a lot of international cases, keeps the placed staffed at all hours to deal with the different time zones. This, however, is Buckinghamshire. International crime isn't much of a thing.

Between curses and banter, Basila talks me through the procedure of installing a back-door with admin privileges.

I almost get it right first time.

I'm not a computer person. A massive fan of technology, don't get me wrong, but I'm basically one generation too far back. Computers were, like, nowhere in the '70s. We had none at school. At all. Try telling the kids of today that and they just won't believe you.

There were a couple at the college. As an art major, I didn't bother with them. It seems weird now when everyone wanders about with enough computing power in their pocket to launch a

NASA moon mission. Back then, and sadly for much of my upbringing, no-one really cared about computers.

I'm a late adopter. The tech has to be run-in before I jump on board. I do know my forward-slash from my back-slash. I've got a couple of little programs stored on my phone that can hack down to a root-drive, rummage out any data I might need.

But in this digital age, let's face it, we all need a Moroccan. Not that she lives in Morocco. Much to the shame of her parents, Basila outed herself as intelligent, and moved to Ramnicu Valcea. A little town in Romania where a few of her fellow cyber-crafters hang out.

She did all of Puppy's new identity and everything for my next iteration. I officially have an older cousin with a daughter. The daughter should be of age in a few years. 'Alexandria' is the name on the birth-certificate. She has school report cards, a doctor's registration, passport, fake social media accounts, the whole nine yards. She's going to come and study with me for a bit and then take over my pottery business.

I'll have to move my base from Elstead to another town.

Bristol has some good galleries, and the West Country is gorgeous. The 'little village' thing is my new addiction. I can keep the London connections going by email and courier, so they won't have to see me in person as I spend the next few years not ageing, then hand everything over to my 'niece'.

That won't be for a while, though.

"Concentrate, you illegitimate daughter of a lesser-known musician! Delete those last four characters and type what I tell you!"

I can't help but smile. "Sorry, Bas."

We go through the last few steps and Basila signs off in a wonderful tirade against the idiot forces of oppression and poor choices in super-hero movie casting, then asks my advice on cooking peppers and lamb mince. I tell her to remember the onions. She says, "Ah! Onions!" and the screen goes blank.

Both Dan and I sit silent for a moment before we realise Bas is gone and our world is considerably freer of inventive curses.

"So," says Dan. "Are all your friends that interesting?"

"Now we're in bed together, so to speak, you're going to have to get used to many of my strange friends, Detective Sergeant Daniel Ripplewater."

"Huh. I'm not sure if I want to know more or less. So, is that it? Is the security of the entire United Kingdom Police Force completely compromised?"

"Technically, but now we just go in and change the password to something Bas doesn't know. Before we leave today, I'll overlay a physical connection key, generate it on this phone, then tuck it away on a USB stick. The backdoor won't open unless a device with the key is plugged in."

"What if I need to change something?"

"Then you'll have to call me. That's what being in bed together means."

That shred of darkness enters his eyes when he realises how dependant on me he will become. I lean in and give him a little nudge and it's amazing. The light shines from him. He has to clamp down on a beaming smile.

"Well, then," he says, "I suppose you'd better give me your number."

"Oh, don't worry, Dan. You're going to get a lot more than my number."

I get to work on finishing the server protocols. Dan sits patiently then begins to doze.

There's a different set of lady's fingerprints to upload to the system, overriding my own (here's one I prepared earlier). I alter the current file on the missing Headless so my mother's name is no longer attached. A formal request goes to the Shengen Server and Interpol to close the file on my 'mother' as the UK police have confirmed her death, certificate attached (another one I prepared earlier). There's a whole procedure to go through with that, but I've flagged it to a separate user account we created for one Detective Constable Tracy Bent-over (sorry, Wendover).

Oh, this is such a relief! I'm buzzing with the possibilities! All the things I can get up to without having to worry if my fucking fingerprints will flag somewhere. Every time they do, I'll get the flag and can kill the investigation with an override.

Oh, frabjous day!

I've been prepping this for years. Ever since I helped Bas escape those Hungarians who had her chained to a chair so she could do all their spam emails. Well, that's a whole other story. Suffice to say, Bas is always happy to help me with my computer issues. And she sends me a card every Christmas. Mostly to point out that she knows where I live.

I'll still be careful not to leave prints. No reason to make extra work for myself.

Bright-Eyes' licence plate is registered to a shell company linked to an international security firm. Dead end. I probably could trace something down through them but there's no point. I have a much, much simpler way, thanks to Dan.

It takes about two hours, all told. Hacking is not a ten second thing like in the movies.

The dopey detective is fast asleep in his chair by the time I'm finished.

Awww, poor boy. He's had a very big day.

Banging my head against the desk would give me the strength to carry him down to the car myself, but that might be difficult to explain to anyone we meet on the way.

Just out of curiosity, I check the browser history, and yep, he googled the Dunwich cottage, checking up on me. Looks like he found the stories I edited.

I shut it all down, make sure I've gathered everything, wipe the workstation and move my chair back to its original spot. Then wipe the chair. There are bits of my fingerprints all over this place. The taps in the men's locker room for a start. It'll take a week for them to notice anything in the computers, if they ever do. If Dan's fingerprints come up in the investigation of the cottage fire, I can change those. By then, dusting this place will be pointless.

The dozing detective gets a little nudge. His head lolls to a comical angle. Another nudge and he starts before waking, looking around, memory supplying the reasons for his location and state of being.

"Sorry. Nodded off."

"And you snored," I lie.

"What? I don't snore."

"Oh! Practically shook the whole building down! Come on. I'll drive."

He has a little moral quandary of a moment before he gets up, wondering exactly what I've done to the system while he rested his eyes. Then I think he remembers that I'm mostly the good guy, even if he doesn't "approve of my methods" and all that nonsense. He ruffles his gorgeous mess of hair and says, "So, where are we going now?"

"My place is too far," I remind him. "After the cottage, your place isn't safe. But don't panic, there are plenty of nice little B&Bs around here we can lose ourselves in."

I almost cringe as I say that, knowing how much of a lie it is, and the extreme unpleasantness that's about to follow. Nothing I can do about that now. I put on a brave face and follow him out of the square brick lump that is Aylesbury Police Headquarters.

Nobody bothers us.

We drive for a few minutes before I spy a clothing bin outside a church. I pull over and grab a small, leather bag, which I stuff with random clothing. Doesn't matter if it fits or not, but we can't turn up to a hotel at three in the morning with only my plastic bag of spare stuff.

Dan catches a few more z's. I can go for hours without sleep, but then I dump and I'm dead to the world. A farm I found on the internet rents bungalows and claims to be open twenty-four hours. They have a vacancy. It looks nice and remote. Hopefully, that'll minimize the chances of anyone else getting hurt.

About half-way there, I pull over next to a row of newer houses on the outskirts of Aylesbury. The bins are lined up ready for collection. I drop the bag containing my bloodied clothes into one at random, leaving Dan's clothes in the back. I might need some leverage if my man gets all pissy about what's going to happen next.

We arrive at the Bed and Breakfast. It's closer to dawn than midnight. The girl behind the counter doesn't seem to mind. She has a stringy frame, weird glasses.

Oh! Why am I dragging this out? Why torture myself? Does it matter if I can remember the girl? If I can describe her in some interesting way?

Fuck it.

I can't cling to these images, lingering on the mundane.

Does it even matter if I remember it all? I'd rather forget. There's so much I'd rather forget. But that's my problem. I hate forgetting. When the beast takes over, I lose whole chunks of my life. And all this is deliberately edited. I don't write down bits I'd rather were different or hadn't happened, amending my life to be kinder, myself to be more competent.

You do realise that none of this actually happened the way I've described, right?

I can't any-more. These holes I have in my life remind me too vividly how inhuman I am. It's not a state I've been able to embrace. It is other. A daemon. A monster. Not part of me. I hate my own nature, so I torture myself by recalling everything in detail.

Like this receptionist. A streak of blue in her goth-black hair. Her lanky awkwardness. That 'anywhere but here' expression on her slack face. The Miyazaki anime she was watching when we came in. Even the particular scent of her chewing gum, a fresh wrapper on the little reception counter.

I did used to be human. Things like her chipped nail varnish still register. Because that matters.

Well, there is a point to remembering all this, I suppose. There is a conversation we had in bed I want to write down. But even that is a form of torture.

I distract Dan by making him fill out the register while I pay for the bungalow with his card. The long streak of a receptionist doesn't even ask for a signature. You don't have to sign with credit cards, just tap. As long as the money clears, no-one cares.

She does show a bit of interest in my man. A protective urge rises. He's not even looking. Shit. I hope Dan's friends are looking. Watching for his card to pop up on the grid. He said they had licenses for that sort of thing.

We head out along the flagstone path to the row of hastily-constructed, plastered, breeze-block 'cottages'. I roll my little suitcase behind me while Dan carries the found bag.

Even at night, the Chilterns are beautiful. A steep hillside opposite contains a lonely house surrounded by lush trees, pale and quiet in the light of the setting moon.

Once inside, we undress and go to bed. Then snuggle. And cuddle. And kiss. And rub and rock and roll. Dan seems happier about it, but he's still too tired, even after his little power-naps. I manage to contain myself to one deep tickle, and the pleasure of watching him try to last a bit longer and failing. He really seems to like me. And he's very nice. Which makes me wonder.

"Why is it you don't have a girlfriend?"

"Huh?"

We're snuggling after, and I'm wondering if he can manage a third time tonight, but I'm too sleepy to really pursue the matter. He's practically dozing off, but makes the effort to chat. Too nice.

"Well, you're a spunk. And you have nice hair, sense of humour. Why no girlfriend?"

"I think it's... I don't know. It's harder to meet girls these days."

"It's easier. Way easier. Fucking Tinder. Ever heard of it?"

"No, that's not what I mean. Harder to make a real connection. Or it's... I think maybe it's easier to isolate yourself, if you want to. Coming back from my Tour, I couldn't process it all. There was a need to bury myself somewhere, let it work itself out. I killed people, shot them, watched them fall. Never saw the bodies up close, though. They wanted me to chat with the army chaplain about it, but I'm not religious and he wasn't a trained psychiatrist, so he didn't help much."

"If the army spends as much as it should on proper psychiatrists and re-integration counselling, they'd have to admit there's a serious problem. It'd hurt their image."

Dan moves slightly away so he can peer down at me and check if I'm being serious. Which I am.

"Huh. Yeah. I suppose. It's kind of a guy-thing, too. You have to hibernate in your cave for a while, if you're a guy."

"No. That's an introvert thing. There are women introverts and men introverts. Trying to separate it by gender is not helpful. Some people just experience things more, or experience more things, and need time to process them. You call it a guy thing because you don't want to admit you have a problem. That's a guy thing. Not wanting to admit you have feelings. Same as the army, because it's run by guys."

"Ha! Yeah." Dan seems genuinely amused by my ramblings. "Right. Sure. Sure. You? How do you cope? With doing something like you just did?"

He wants me to reassure him that it'll all get better. He picked the wrong girl for that.

"I don't cope. I don't think there is any coping. I'm just fucked up. I have my art. Occasional tantrums. Alcohol. Sex is useful." I give him a little tickle. "I write about it, too. The pages go straight onto the fire afterwards so they're never found, but putting it down on paper helps."

I shift onto my back so I can think clearer, hooking his arm behind my head for a pillow.

"Maybe that makes it seem more normal, ordinary somehow. A story that's happening to someone else. The writing's terrible. I can never remember if I've already included a little detail or if I've told a bit of the story before, or if some side point is actually relevant, so I end up repeating myself." (Yeah. This.) "And wandering off on tangents. I don't know. It doesn't seem to affect me like it should. Because I have trouble making new memories, I don't think it scars my brain the same. You'd have to ask someone in neuroscience. Er. Yeah. Never mind."

Damn. See? This is the problem. I just gave too much away. Not good.

"What do you mean you have trouble making new memories?"

I really don't want to have to kill him. Keep the bullshit simple, see if he swallows it.

"It's just a thing. Short term to long term memory disconnect. I had a whole bunch of tests done. They couldn't find anything wrong with me. They wanted to take some blood, but that's impossible." Ah! Fuck! No! Stop! I'm too relaxed, not keeping proper control of my mouth. "I don't want any of my DNA floating around, just in case. Sounded like a lot of psycho-babble to me, anyway. They used a lot of fancy terms to say I'm a bit of a scatterbrain."

"So, you never wanted a normal life?"

"I do. I have a normal life. I love my pottery. But I also have a very extra hobby. Like skydiving, or whatever. You, soldier boy, you try really hard to be normal. Is that because you know you're not?"

He sighs, getting sleepier. "Maybe. Probably. I really wanted kids when I was in my early twenties but I could never, um, lure them into my car."

"Ha! Funny bastard." I nudge him, but we're both too tired to get anything going again. "I don't think either of us were built for normal. Maybe that's why we connect."

He grunts. Oh, poor boy. Sooooo tired. I guess we can try and pick this conversation up after. After, after, after. If he sees too much, it's going to be a very different conversation. But hey. Morning will reveal all.

# 11

# Factory

I wake up, head heavy. Fuzzy. Something's not right. I was dreaming about... Wow.

A bright yellow bus, bending into a curve to follow this impossibly narrow track, climbing around and around the thinnest mountain spire of psychedelic ice-cream, trying to get to the cherry on top. The moonlight cast a rainbow and the stars were dancing a full-on Rogers and Hammerstein routine. The bus propelled itself by merrily eating the road and shitting out exhaust like a rocket while I sat in a silver bikini with a monster growing out of the hole under my left breast, all purple and green, slimy and phallic.

Shit.

Drugs.

They fucking drugged me.

Idiots. I was going to come anyway.

I'm dressed in what I slept in. Panties and a singlet.

Someone's crying. A girl. Stupid bitch needs to shut the fuck up or she's going to get my very unsympathetic fist in her whimpering face.

Something is very wrong. I need water, but there's none here.

Shit, what is this? A stash-house? Prostitutes are moved from city to city, sold by one group of gangsters to another. Johns get tired of fucking the same old girls. There are stash-houses all up and down England, for girls and drugs and guns and whatever can be held by the larger gangs. I'm guessing this is some place that belongs to the Midlands mob who operate out of Birmingham.

I was in a place like this, briefly. Many, many years ago. Before they took me to be prepared. Before that red-domed room swallowed me whole. Flashbacks from when I was still human, terrified and alone, snatched from outside college, dragged into a van. The room was smaller than this. I cried, like that whimpering bitch.

Huh. This is weird. I want to open my eyes but can't. That's the opposite of what usually happens. Usually, I don't want to open my eyes but I have to.

No, wait.

There's something on my face. A bag? No, a blindfold. Oh, this is just ridiculous. Who uses a fucking blindfold? My wrists are tied with rope, my hands in front of me. That's probably what's twisting my insides, the tied wrists. That's how they restrained me for my ordeal. Way back when they made me.

It was some place underground, a deep chamber tiled in red. Men dragged me down the stairs, around and around, down and down. I thought they were going to rape me. They did, but it was worse than that. They stripped me naked, pulled my hands up over my head.

I'm getting the shakes.

That's not right.

Deep breaths. Take it easy.

I'm not a little girl any more, not a virgin sacrifice. I wasn't even a virgin at the time, though I told everyone I was. Steve Plimsole. Nasty little boy got me drunk and I let him. A couple of times. That weekend when his parents were away. We were never really going out.

And I'm all grown up now.

Cold and calculating, that's me. Even with my hands tied in front of me. Dumb way to restrain someone who knows what they're doing. How the fuck do they think that's going to stop me? I suppose the whole idea is that they really don't know who they're fucking with.

The smell of the concrete floor is distinct. Old and industrial. More fucking concrete. I mean, it's not like I was expecting a feather bed and shag-pile carpet. I'm not chasing Bond villains, here. I had my fill of concrete at the police station.

There are other odours. Urine, long dried, the sharp sting of human sweat, and something like a cross between vinegar and rubber. Probably black-tar heroine.

Like all blindfolds, this one does a pretty poor job of blocking my vision. It's literally just a piece of cloth tied over my eyes. My nose lifts the bottom section far enough away for me to peer through.

The only light comes from a single bulb, caged in heavy glass and metal, bolted to one wall. It casts strange shadows, giving the whole room a film-noir feel.

Some haggard, sagging junkie with greying hair is dissolving her heroine, diluting it prior to shooting up.

Black Tar is really low quality. The impurities are what give it that colour, texture and consistency. It's probably the dregs of the gang's production. The ratty stuff they can't sell, so they give it to their girls to keep them strung out and compliant.

The mattress she's sitting on is dumped straight onto the floor, though there is a sheet and blanket.

The whimpering comes from the other occupant. A vaguely pretty girl, she's finishing up her shot, head sinking back as she relaxes her arm and lets the needle slide out, sniffling at where her life has led. A newcomer to this lower state of existence, she hates being reminded how far she's sunk, that she's now a drug-addicted whore, and cries when she injects.

Her despairing sobs cut into me like a knife.

I was like that, once. I lay on a floor, weeping in terror and begging my daddy to come find me. He never did. Left long before I was taken. Left me and mother and never came back. Dying is such a selfish act. I was lost, alone, completely helpless. Didn't know how to fight, or even that I could fight. And the robes and chanting, it all numbed my brain, so I couldn't think what to do.

Now, I my chest tightens again, lip trembling in sympathy. The tears start leaking. No. No sympathy for her. I can't let my humanity in, let it distract me just because I've found a decent fuck.

Where the hell is Dan?

The whore whimperer leans back and mutters, "Apu, apu..." as she fades into her dreams. "Daddy, Daddy."

My gut wrenches in response. I guess I'll have to work with that.

I give a moan and shift, jerk at my restraints. A little panicked squeal when I find that I can't move my hands. As I flail, trying to remove the blindfold, the old whore chides me.

"You don't wanna to do that, love. Just piss 'em off, you will. Get what they gave her."

She nods at the other girl and I twist my head about to get a better look from under the blinding band. Oh, shit, there's blood on the side of her head. Damaging the goods. That's just stupid. They'll want to get her out to work as quick as possible. Are they amateurs? Or did she do something really bad?

My upset state makes an excellent cover for being all panicked and clueless. That's usually the best way to get people to overshare.

"Oh, fuck, what did they do? Where am I?" My voice is genuinely thick with emotion. "Please, I don't know where I am or how I got here. Please."

"You'se at the cement factory, darlin', right down in the cellar, so don't put on that innocent act with me. This is the fuckin' shithole. Darkest of the dark. We's in the old quarry. Miles from anywhere." She uses the needle to swirl the heroine solution around in a small, plastic cup. "Scream all you like kinda deal. Who'd ya piss off ta get sent down 'ere, then?"

"I don't know! I don't know anyone to piss off. What's going on? Please. Oh, god, help me! HELP! HEEEELP!"

I'm sick of waiting. I have to get away from this sobbing bitch, cutting into my soul. Let's get this party started, and get me back to lying about how powerful and intelligent I am.

"Don't fuckin' yell!" says the old whore. "Not so fuckin' loud, love. Keep it down or we's all gettin' in trouble. Think you'se an upstairs girl?" She syringes up the horrific looking liquid. "Like any of these fuckin' pigs care about you? Ooo, you'se in for a helluva shock." She trails off as she focuses on her task, the rising anticipation of a hit. "This is the hole, love. The fuckin' hole. Fuck, bitch..."

Her warnings come too late. Footsteps, the click of a padlock, a clunk as the bolt is retracted, then the door swings in.

Both the other women make themselves small, curl away, not wanting to be noticed. From the greyness of an underground room lit by distant lights, a short but stocky man enters. Trackie-Daks and a wife-beater singlet.

"Ona śpi," he yells back over his shoulder. Polish. Fuck, I hardly know any Polish. I think he said, 'She's awake'. That's more from context than anything else.

He's wearing gloves. Work-gloves, like gardening gloves but used by workmen. Are they loading? Mixing a batch? I thrash my head about trying to get a good look at him from under the blindfold, clutching my hands to my chest like a good little frightened girl.

Shit.

How long do I have to keep up this crap? It's really getting to me. There are actual tears on my face. Fuck's sake.

Wife-Beater takes a step into the room and a harsh, almost panicked cry, "Ostrożny!" comes from the outer room. Someone wants him to be careful. Wife-Beater looks at me and snorts in derision. However, he shuffles from the room, closing the door, bolting it. *Clunk.* The padlock goes back on. *Click.*

"Shit, love. Thought we was all for the fuckin' hose then!" The old whore half cackles in fear at how close she came. "That's..." and she tells me his name, but I've already settled on Wife-Beater, so I do my best to forget it. "Nasty fucker, that one. Do you do anal, love?"

"Anal...? Sex? Anal sex? No! I've never...!"

"Won't be able to say that after tonight, love! Likes goin' up a nice, tight, young arse does that one." She cackles joyfully again, and the sniveller starts sniffling afresh. "But don't worry about it. This is what ya fuckin' want." She waves her filled needle about, a lethargic triumph of small joy. "They won't give ya this upstairs. Too dirty. But I fuckin' love it. I misbehaves on purpose, just so they send me here and I can get this shit. I'm gettin' past me use-by date. Not got much longer to go. So I's gotta take me pleasures where I can. Don't like that pure shit. Even the cut shit. This is my fix. The darkest, most horrible crap you can get."

She cackles again, genuinely pleased with herself.

"Meglehetősen!" The weeping woman whimpers. Shut up.

Now, that's Hungarian, a language you definitely want to learn if you get mixed up in the human trafficking business. The old hag cackles louder. I'm not sure if it's out of spite or even if the old dear understood or not.

"Hagyd abba a nevetést..." Pretty continues. Something about not laughing, but the whimperer trails off on the last word, high already.

It's not even the Hungarians. They're just couriers. It's the Italians via Hungary and other places. Fucking Mafia, constantly buying new girls for their high-end prostitution rackets, keeping the politicians and authorities happy so they can operate with impunity.

Maybe the weeper started young, and is in shock at being removed from her position of privileged fucker. Thought she was an old-fashioned courtesan. Now she's finding out why you don't reply to those emails telling you about how to become a model, or looking for dancers in the Eastern Bloc.

Whatever. Fuck that bitch. I'm not going to cry. It might be inhumanly unsympathetic but I'm not human. Not anymore. I'm the avatar for a daemon that delights in my pain. She's just a stupid whore.

There are a thousand girls like her, a million tales of women who think they'll get somewhere by letting someone else use them. Then they find out the person was just using them and had no intention on delivering. It's not a narrative I've ever supported. If you want something, go get it for yourself.

Meanwhile, I'm flexing hard against the rope. They've gone a bit overboard. Four or five loops wrapped around going some way up my forearm. I wrench at it, getting my shaking breath under control. The rope stretches, little by little, creating more space between my wrists. Keep the hands jammed outwards, so it looks at though the rope is still tight. It'll take a little while before it's loose enough for me to get some velocity into it and tear the rope.

Oh. Here they come.

A horde of them.

Sounds of activity outside the room indicate there are many men gathered to drag this one, poor little girl to her fate. Me. I mean, drag me to my fate. While I'm pretending to be a poor little girl.

Four of them enter. I wave my head about in tearful terror, trying to get a look at them in the dim room from under my inadequate blindfold, whimpering away.

I flinch and twist, struggling weakly as they lay hands on my bare arms and bare legs. Keep the wrists taut. Don't spoil the surprise. They're rough about it, lifting me off the ground and, one to a limb, hauling me out into a larger space.

Finally.

No more sobbing girl in the cellar. I can get back to my new self.

It's some kind of basement under the factory, just like the old whore said. Not that big. They carry me past tables where they're sorting... Something. Packages. Money? Drugs? Ammunition? All three? There are lights on each of the tables, and dim daylight filters down the steps, but I'm blocked by the men and a stupid blindfold, so I can't see properly.

I'd say they carried me up the stairs but then I'd be missing the perfect opportunity to use the word 'manhandled'. They keep muttering cautionary admonishments to each other. Their grips are tight. It's almost like they're afraid of me. I twist about and plead with them a bit, just for show.

The first landing holds some battered looking pressure tanks scattered about. What does that say? N2O? Oh, fucking laughing gas. Criminals pump this into houses before they rob them, thinking it'll knock out any victims who are home. This is what gave me such vivid and interesting dreams. Mostly useless, but slightly effective in a trailer or small cottage, like the one I rented with Dan's card.

How much did they use? It takes a ton of alcohol to affect me. Half a bottle of your finest spirits and I'll feel a little buzz. Maybe I'm particularly susceptible to inhanlents. I'll have to buy some crack and test that.

I'm still shaking. Fuck. Why can't I get this shaking under control?

Oh, Dan! Shit!

Where the fuck is the dopey detective in all of this?

We come up into the factory proper. The place certainly has seen better days. Foliage presses in at almost every window. Wooden pallets of various wrapped illegalities sit in little clusters among the rusted, iron pillars. The roof looks well patched. One wall, farthest from the door, contains a row of shipping containers. I can't get a good look because of the bandage over my eyes, but it appears they have added basic plumbing.

Holiday cottages they call them. For storing the girls who don't misbehave. That's more the sort of place I was kept. With strict instructions no one was to touch the virgin.

A cluster of men sit at a small table in front of them, playing cards. Squinting, I see at least one gun tucked into a waistband.

They don't take me down that far, instead wheel me around towards a large, high room built into the side of the factory. Oh, it's a loading bay, large enough to have two cement trucks parked in at once, broken roller-doors looking out over the drop into the quarry.

We're on the raised platform, like a stage, about six metres wide, maybe twice as long. More. All the equipment has gone. It's just a shell. This is old industry, crumbling in the Midlands as it's moved to a cheaper north, then offshore. It's been replaced by a new industry of feeding the poor to the rich.

No holiday pay or maternity leave required.

"Pyotr!" one of them calls as they enter the space. "Where you want this one?" English. Broken, accented English. Huh.

"Bring her over here," a Brummie accent answers. "Put her on the bar." The speaker elongates baaaar, like it's some amazing thing I should terrify me. But I don't know what it is, so...

I'm carried over to something hanging from a roof beam.

Wait, is there more than one person here?

I'm surrounded and being twisted about, so it's difficult to see.

They spread my legs. Someone welded a metal bar to the floor of the loading bay. There are metal tracks, probably for moving the spout into position, but all the tanks and equipment for filling the cement trucks are long gone. The same smartarse cut a pair of handcuffs and welded one half to each side of the bar, making for some damned uncomfortable leg shackles.

I think it's meant to emphasise their dominance over me, spreading my legs like this. There's a chain dangling from a metal I-beam holding up the roof. When my hands are hauled skyward and firmly attached, a new stench wafts over and pulls off my blindfold.

It's a fucking disappointment. I was expecting Bright-Eyes in his Armani, but no, it's just some ugly punk.

If I was standing normally, we'd probably be about the same height. As it is, he tries his best to loom over me and snarl, all intimidating.

"Oh, no, no," I whimper. Getting sick of that, too. "Please, please don't hurt me. Please, I don't know anything."

I'm guessing his name is actually Peter. This one I don't mind remembering because I'm sure he really has it coming. Tattoos on both arms and across his exposed chest, a spider-web on the neck. So original.

I swing my vison around in fear, looking for an escape, taking in the bench along the back wall, covered in various tools. Is that a fucking samurai sword?

My desperate state seems to please Peter, who smiles at his men, revealing gold-plated teeth. Chuckles ensue. Peter flicks the ring of keys he has clipped through a belt loop, swaggering on the spot in anticipation. Of all the people here, he's the one with the longest hair. The others are close cropped clones in slightly varied sportswear. Peter has a patch shaved on one side with, you guessed it, a tattoo underneath. The other side is jet black and has a tendancy to flop forward over one eye.

I look over his shoulder. Tied to a chair is poor, dopey Dan, looking decidedly the worse for wear. Tragic little soldier.

Fuck, this is just, this is so fucked. Right after we had that whole conversation about torture not working. The people I'm chasing don't want to get their hands dirty. They think Dan and I did the cottage together, killed all their friends and burned them. Ma'am's boys want to find out what we know, but they're so fucking paranoid about getting involved, getting uncovered. They've handed us over to some local mobsters to extract the information.

This is the problem with modern Britain. Everything is delegated and distributed to protect everyone involved, to the point where nobody actually knows what the fuck is going on.

These laughable idiots are so convinced it's Dan who knows things. They're beating him up because he's the MAN, and must be in charge.

Ridiculous.

Dan raises his head and squints through one eye. The other is swollen shut. He sees me and tries not to react, but I can see it hurts him. *Don't worry, little soldier boy. I'll get you out. I'm so, so sorry. I'll make it up to you later. A lot. I promise.*

There could be outfits.

"You can drop the act, love. We've been warned about you."

Ironic, isn't it? They're going to tell me what I want to know. Almost funny.

"Please! Please, no! You've got the wrong person! I don't, I don't know anything! Pleeeease!"

Peter punches my pleading face and I can barely keep myself from grinning as I feel the daemon rising in earnest, my head singing with ecstacy. I flash back to the cackling old whore in the basement. 'Ooo, you'se in for a helluva shock.' Well, not me, but somebody.

Dan cries out and tries his bonds.

Peter laughs at him. "Ha! Yeah. Now you'll fuckin' talk, won't you?"

But he can't, because Dan doesn't really know anything. Idiots.

The Polish thugs wander over the bench and pick up various heavy, sharp things. Peter flicks his keys and swaggers. Wife-Beater grabs himself a pair of long-handled tin-snips. One of them wanders towards me with a hammer. Peter yanks my hair back, staring down into my face. I kindly bend my knees so the fucking shrimp can do that.

"And you won't be able to pull any of your fuckin' tricks, neither." He grabs the hammer and presses the claw-side into my cheek. "We've been warned all about you, bitch."

Oh, please. If you knew all about me, you'd be too terrified to be in the same room.

Then I spy my handbag on the table, lining all ripped up and it's enriched guts spilled out. Gun, taser, ties, lighter, my precious phone, the lot.

Shit.

I'm not sure this act of mine is really fooling anyone, but I've started so I may as well carry on, see if I can get anyone to crack. From anger if not ego.

I try to keep the fear in my eyes. No doubt they're still red from crying. The windows to the soul are a great place to put up false advertising.

"Dan? Oh, Dan, Dan! What's going on? Dan, are you... Oh, what have they done to you?"

"Never mind what we've done to him! You should be worried about what I'm going to do to you with this fuckin' hammer! Then Serge gets to use his sword."

Cheap knock-off. I wouldn't disgrace the name Katana by using that term for this piece of tat. A soft alloy version sold to tourists. They've sharpened it. Clumsily.

Oooo, scary.

"We're all going to take turns! And if your stupid git of a boyfriend still doesn't talk, I'm going to use THIS," he presses the claws deeper into my cheek and his face up against mine, "to hammer a couple of fuckin' nails into your cunt! From the front! Then we're all going to take turns fuckin' you in your new hole!"

I'm so tempted to say, 'You have a penis the size of a nail?' but that would ruin the moment. It's really hard to keep the daemon at bay, but I want some information before they get to see my bad side. I have to get the focus off Dan or he may not survive this.

"Is this because of The Lady? I didn't hear her name, I swear! They just called her Ma'am! That's all I heard them say, The Lady and Ma'am!" Peter looks confused, but somebody tenses up. "Please! I don't know anything about her!" Which one of them was it?

"Ma'am? Don't know any fucking Ma'am. The only bitches I know are-"

"Wait, wait. How you know this name?" Oh, it's Serge with the sword. We have a winner.

"I don't know her name, I just, they were talking-" You tell me her name. Come on.

"Talk? Who fuckin' talk?"

"Serge?" Tattooed Pete seems confused. "What's she on about?"

"Shut the fuck up, man!" Serge moves in with his big, shiny weapon. Oh, he's invested. Maybe they told him he could be part of the cabal if he proved himself. Like they'd ever let some dirty foreigner into their club. He's hooked, though. Fantastic. And I can see the bulge of two phones in his pocket. Doubtless unlocked by his thumbprint. I'll have to remember to leave his thumbs attached.

Peter doesn't like being reminded he's not top dog. "Don't you fuckin' tell me to shut up!"

"Just chill the fuck out, man." Serge's friends move into a different pattern, one focussed around Peter. They seem confused by Serge, so not part of the inner circle, but back him up without hesitation.

Mr Tattoo has a sudden twitch of fear and doesn't know what to say or who to wave his hammer at.

Serge looks really angry, shaking the sword in my face. "Who say this name? You tell right fuckin' now!"

Calmly I reply, "So. You're the one I need to talk to. Nice to meet you, Serge."

Now Serge seems confused, but his confusion only fuels his anger. "You tell me!" he yells, drawing back the sword. "I cut your fuckin' legs off, bitch!"

Serge swings low and hard into my left shin. I tense. The sword judders and he nearly drops it. The sharpness gives me a wave of the sun.

Imagine bathing in the light of a thousand electric orgasms and you're not even close!

Fuck, I nearly lost it.

Got to keep it together. Can't rip them apart. Yet.

I've had some recent practice in not losing it, thanks to Dan and his serving of orgasms.

Serge checks the blade with his thumb and promptly cuts himself. "Ai!" He looks at me with even greater confusion. That feeds even more anger.

Oh, but he's furious now!

He steps in, winds up and hacks repeatedly at my thigh. Two, three massive hits before the cheap, alloy sword snaps at the handle and the blade flies off, everyone flinching in shock.

Needless to say, there's not a mark on me, though I might get a bit of a bruise later.

"Oh, it's true!" says Peter "You're *her*. Holy fuck! The stories are all true!"

"No, Peter," I tell him. "The stories are a load of bullshit."

I pulse both legs and the handcuff shackles around my ankles snap from their welds. It's not just the big, slow-twitch fibres in my muscles that the daemon enhances. It's the fast twitch fibres, too.

"Nobody knows the truth," I tell Peter.

I lash out and wrap both legs around Serge the Surprised. One of the Poles starts crossing himself. Like that's going to help.

"Not even me. But together..."

I pull down on the chain, curl up and toss Serge high into one distant wall. He screams until he hits with a wet thud, then falls all the way down to the floor crunching and gasping, alive and useful.

Can't lose it.

Must keep him alive.

"...together, Peter my friend, we're all going to try and get a little closer to the truth."

I relax my wrists and yank my hands free of the rope and chain, stretching my arms wide and shaking loose while they all cry out or swear quietly, readying their various impotent weaponry.

"Fuck. You're not even human."

"Oh! Dan!"

I forgot about him. He's sitting there, one eye half swollen shut but the other open wide, stark realisation on his battered face.

"...um... Hi. Yeah. Sorry. Not really human any-more. Did I not mention that?"

# 12

# Quarry

"Pierdol sie kurwo!" ...something about a fucking whore...
Oh, yeah. I have to deal with these guys.
"Hold that thought," I tell Dan.
Three of the other Polish thugs are in a little cluster. There's one straggler. Serge shifts, but then screams with a muffled, grinding sound of broken bones. He's not getting up any time soon.
My bare feet get a reasonable grip on the dusty, concrete floor, but I won't be able to really show off. I'm not sure how willing Dan is to be an audience, but that's the advantage of him being tied to a chair. Again. Maybe it'll become a whole thing, where I have to tie him down to get excited and-
*FOCUS, GIRL!*
Baddies.
Right.
Two blindingly fast steps and I'm in the middle of the cluster, shaping up on Wife-Beater for a side-kick. I do practice my Kung-Fu outside the morning BaGua classes. Meng Laoshi does private lessons. Being an ex-ballet dancer gives me the flexibility. Forty years of constant practice gives me the muscle memory. My little

woodland walks lead to some secluded areas where I've kicked the shit out of the trees.

The impact cracks something in Wife Beater's sternum. Rather than flying away across the room, he kind of folds around the kick in a most unnatural manner, then sits hard.

This gives Wrench-Boy a chance to swing at me. Instead of retracting from the kick, I curl under the plumber's tool, grabbing it in one hand, pulling and continuing the circular motion of the swing, but wider to take him off balance, then sharply narrowing the radius to break his wrist.

I take the wrench from his limp grip and continue the circle, swinging up to smash his companion in the chin, lifting him off his feet, folding his entire jaw up behind his overbite, through the roof of his mouth, and into his brains.

Ba-Gua-Zhang is all about using circles, maintaining momentum.

With the wrench held high, I continue the spin and return it to its original owner, albeit sticking out of his head.

The straggler has run up to the fray by this point but stutters in hesitation at my calm demeanour and his destroyed companions.

I step up to him directly.

Xing Yi Quan is all about directness of action. It's a complementary style to BaGua. They're often studied together.

Slipping inside his guard, I punch Straggler in the jaw, a nice left cross that dislocates both sides in a loud snap, precipitating his collapse into unconsciousness.

All the while, the beast is twisting and snarling inside me, tearing at its chains.

As I stroll over to Dan, I comment, "Relatively sedate, by my standards, don't you think?"

Peter points his hammer at me. "...you..."

Dan glances at him, then down at his chair. It's made of square metal tubing with bits of handcuffs welded all over it, and is, of itself, welded to the tracks. Probably custom built by one of this lot.

Painted Pete is getting his ego up to the task, but it's proving awkward for him, "...you are not... fuck."

"Are you okay?" I ask Dan. "Show me the eye." Hhe flinches back as I gently reach in. "Oh, stop that," I admonish, playfully slapping his arm.

Dan takes a panicked breath then, wonder of wonders, he relaxes. Exhaling in relief he sits there panting slightly, a rueful smile tugging at his lips. I have good look.

"Not that bad," I tell him. "You won't have any deep scarring."

I give him a little peck on the cheek.

"I seem to be all tied up again," Dan says apologetically. "It's like we have a special song, already."

I smile and try to think of something inappropriate to say, but Peter insists on interrupting.

"You are not going to be the fuckin' end of me, bitch!" The hammer twitches in rhythm to his mantra. "You are not fuckin' ending me!"

"Just a second," I say to Dan.

Sliding back, I turn and kick Peter in the balls. One of them bursts, his pelvis cracks, a couple of organs rupture inside and he's lifted a good fifteen centimetres off the ground. Stepping in, I whip out one hand and unclip his keys as he collapses. A long, high-pitched whine, like a kettle dying, escapes his lips. He slips into unconsciousness from the extreme pain. He'll bleed to death internally.

Returning to my man, I flick through until I find the little key for handcuffs. I undo the ones around my ankles first.

"Wow. They didn't even leave a mark on you," Dan comments.

"No. I don't get marked up," I say as I start on his various restraints. "So you can slap me about as much as you dare."

"Not going to be that much."

"Wise man. It also makes donating blood difficult."

He gently rubs the spot on my naked leg where the sword hit, fascinated. I'm not sure if he means it to be as arousing as it is.

"There's a little mark here," he says.

"Well, I do get bruises sometimes, but they always fade. I don't know how or why they form. Why they leave."

Oh, such a relief that I have someone I can talk to! I'll have to see how it pans out over the next couple of days, but he's not lost it yet.

"It's something to do with that medical strip on your chest, isn't it?"

"Let's chat about this later. I've got to go through Serge's multiple phones and get him to sing." I give him a little wink. "Cross-reference."

Dan snorts a resigned agreement while I finish uncuffing him. He's a bit slow getting to his feet, obviously in a lot of pain.

The first of the gunshots goes well wide of us both.

"Look out!" Dan cries, pushing me out of the way.

Idiot.

I kick his feet out from underneath him and he goes down hard. Standing quickly, I move to cover him with my body as more shots come, a second shooter joining in.

Stamping one of my feet horizontally onto a heavy metal leg of the chair, I launch myself at the doorway.

It's not like I forgot about the four men from the other room, I just didn't expect them to pay any attention to all the screaming. I'm sure there's usually a lot of screaming. Maybe it was the sudden absence of screaming.

Okay, look. I got distracted by my man and the joys of killing Peter by rupturing his groin. Perhaps I am the idiot.

In MMA fights this is called a 'Superman Punch'. My trajectory is longer, flatter and faster than is traditional for such an attack. Plus, my fist punches a hollow cave into shooter's head, which I've never seen happen in the ring, but is totally what would happen if a man made out of steel or with one with super-speed or even a metallic, armoured suit-

Okay. Let's just say I'm not a fan of superhero movies.

I land and use both hands to swing the man on the end of my fist around in a flat arc, knocking the other shooter back.

The remaining two snuck up for a look, unarmed, and are now back-pedalling furiously. I pick up a fallen gun and empty it into both of them. The slide hasn't been oiled properly. The mechanism scratches as it operates. Poorly maintained. Browning Hi-Power by the looks of it. Good enough to get the job done.

My strength gives me a nice, steady firing platform. I don't think any of the shots carried as far as the containers. The girls inside should be safe. I'll check on them later.

The second shooter shifts groggily on the floor. I throw the gun through his head and he goes down.

I've always been good at throwing things.

Returning to Dan, there's a dark pool growing under his chest. I hesitate in my step, suddenly unable to breathe. He shifts and sees me, eyes alert, conscious. The hole is low down on the right-hand side. Top of the liver by the darkness of the blood. From the sound of his breathing, the shot also tore open the bottom of his lungs.

"Hey. Did you get 'em?" he asks, agony in his voice, a bubbling sound as the blood fills his chest cavity.

"What?"

"The bad guys. Did you g-" Blood rises into his throat. He coughs. "Oh, shit. Got clipped. Don't worry. I think it was a through and through. Look. You're going to have to find something to wad up the, the holes. Quick as you can. Drop me at a hospital. Don't worry, I won't... Won't say nothing..."

"Anything."

"Huh?"

"You won't say anything."

"Yeah, yeah. Fucking grammar nazi on top of being an alien."

"I'm not an alien!"

"Whatever, just, quick as you can. Get something, anything, shirts, anything."

I pace over, my steps heavy, eyes stinging. "Oh, Dan! I'm so sorry."

"Yeah, yeah. Never mind all that, just, something. Find-" *cough* "-something to plug the holes. Docs can patch me up."

"You're bleeding badly. The hole in the back is bigger than the little one in the front. It's..." I look at the fear hiding behind his eyes. "You might have a couple of minutes."

"You. You can stop it. Just. Just find something..." His words grow weaker. "...oh, fuck, this hurts..."

"It's okay. It's okay." I crouch and take his hand. "I'll fix you. I'll fix it all. Oh, Dan, Dan. Yours was a sad life of loneliness, loyalty betrayed by the army, the very people you served with. You isolated yourself from everyone, even those you were still trying to protect. A hero. A real hero, that's what you are. I'll help you rebuild your faith in the world, liar that I am. I won't lie to you, Dan. I swear. I'll stay true to you."

That's exactly what I said. Word for word.

He's gone. Eyes dim. He had seconds, not minutes. The rate he was bleeding, nothing I could do. The hepatic vein was severed, gushing. The heart goes into shock and arrests.

One stray shot. One little bullet and a man who might have been able to accept me is gone from the world.

At least I said all I wanted to say to him, comforted him properly. I said everything right and didn't go to pieces. No crying. It's not like I was kneeling next to him and screaming his name in fury and despair. I would never do that.

I'm not crying now, as I write this.

What did I do next?

I sniffed, looking up, blinking. Got to keep it together. Work to be done. There's a gun with my fingerprints all over it inside that man's head. Need to clean that.

A deep shudder begins and I rock back on my heels, onto my arse, hands flailing onto the floor. No, no. Keep it together. Keep looking up. Keep breathing. I have work. So much work to do.

But first.

Serge managed to slide all the way across the loading platform and down into the driveway on his broken leg. He thinks he can hide at the end of his blood trail.

I head over to the edge of the dock, stopping there as I peer at him dragging along the ground. Staring down at him. Burning.

The daemon surges.

No.

I can't let these feelings flash into murderous ecstasy. Not right now. But I'm burning. Burning so fiercely inside. Maybe, from where he's cowering, Serge can see that on my face.

You can't just torture people. You have to break them completely.

Eventually, what's left of Serge tells me everything I need to know. I cross-reference with the texts on his multiple phones, unlocked by his thumbprint.

Once he's no longer able to scream, I get bored and head back into the factory.

They drove my boring old Corolla up here. I can see it from the loading bay. The keys are on the table with the rest of my stuff. I pick up my phone, gun, making sure to stamp on the head of the guy I left unconscious with the broken jaw.

It's just the lining they tore out of the bag. I can fix that. I wanted to make some alterations anyway, improvements to the hidden pockets.

I chuck all my stuff inside, lining be damned, and head downstairs. With some holes cut in my blindfold I pull it down so I can wear it like a mask. They were separating money into packets. That's why they had the work-gloves on. To avoid paper-cuts from the cash.

Paper-cuts are the worst.

And even at that idea of pain, I stop, doubling over, crying out, almost overwhelmed with a sudden grief.

No, no, no. This isn't like me at all. I don't have feelings. I'm cold calculating and sobbing on my knees, clutching my bag. I cry for so long that tears soak through my blindfold-mask, form a small pool on the concrete. No, this can't be me. I look up, but then curl all the way over in a fresh wave of sobbing.

It passes.

I look at the money. The drugs. That's way more than I spent on petrol. But I don't want any of it. Fucking nothing to do with any of this shit.

It takes a moment, and then even that, too, passes. Time does not bring relief. You have all lied, who told me time would ease me of my pain. Good old Edna Millay. Time cannot heal me because I can never be hurt. Ha. My daemon preserves my physical body so the beast can feed on all my other pain. Pure fucking evil.

Time passes.

On with the show.

I pretend to need a crowbar to free the rest of the girls from the shipping containers. They flee through the room were Serge and I had our conversation. Good luck getting a clean footprint from that mess. Some of the girls flinch and squeal. I think one of them actually vomits. That's okay. Sometimes, I vomit at the sight of my handiwork.

The old whore grabs as much of the drugs as she can carry and bolts. She'll be dead from an overdose within a week.

A couple of the girls look grateful, desperate and together enough. Well, about as together as I am right now. I give them the keys to the Corolla, help them load it with cash, and tell them of a lady I know in the Spanish Pyrenees, at a resort town east of San Sebastian. She might be able to set them up.

That'll be a road trip with some interesting stories.

I give my hands, arms, legs, and face a quick splashing in one of the sinks. There's a lot of blood splatter.

My girl, Puppy, should be around somewhere. It's called pranking, where you let the phone ring twice and then hang up.

Headlights flash from the other side of the quarry.

It takes me a while to walk around. I only have to stop once and have an outburst of feelings. Then I'm back together. Walking without crying. It's a bit of scrabble up the side at the end. They had bottles of water for the girls, and I grabbed a couple, but I'm hungry by the time I arrive at the Nissan Leaf. She's parked at the end of some farm track that's been interrupted by the quarry's old expansion.

Puppy's not there.

I sniff and wipe my face. "It's okay, Puppy, I'm alone!"

A patch of bushes along the edge of the quarry shifts and my blue-haired angel emerges, shedding bits of brush and grass she used to break up the line of her body, clicking on the safety of her DSR1 Precision Sniper Rifle, chambered in .338 Lapua Magnum. I don't know guns; I'm just reading off my notes. It's smaller than a normal sniper rifle because it's a bullpup design. That means the chamber is behind the trigger not in front of it. German made. She picked it because my Hungarian contacts know where to get the ammunition easily. Puppy loves her toy. She's effective up to two-hundred metres. It's a shame this isn't a story where you'll get to see her use it.

I know, I know. Chekov's Sniper Rifle. But no.

"Did you keep checking behind me, like I taught you?"

She wanders over and beeps the car unlocked. "Yeah, yeah. Just a few girls. Three drove off. The rest all clump together carrying their bundles, and wander the road."

"*Clumped* together and *wandered-*"

"Ugh. Past tense, fuck you." She strips off the silencer, hinges up the back seat and stows it all underneath. She's altered the battery casing to act as a carry. The seat bed has sprung carbon-fibre slats above to create enough space and still make the bench comfortable. Fuck an engineering student and they'll do all kinds of modifications to your car. "Clumped together and wandered the road. No. To the road. Down the road? To or down?"

"Down would be better. You might say, wandered off down the road."

"Sure, sure. I'll get it. I just need to watch more TV." She gets a cheeky little half-smile. "Lots and lots of TV." She opens the driver's side door.

"You need to study!" I retort.

"Yeah, yeah. Spare clothes in the back. You can lecture me once you have some pants on. The fuck is that on your face? A blindfold, or something?"

There's even a wet towel. I trained my Puppy well. Now, I can take my mask off. Once I'm freshly dressed, I climb into the passenger seat.

"Ah! You look better!"

Puppy grins at me like it's all game. Just some stupid, silly game. She flips the back seat down. I nearly crack it completely. My breath slips out of control, my hands wander, to my seatbelt buckle, to the dashboard, not knowing what to do.

Maybe, maybe it is just that. A silly game. What the fuck does any of it matter? Like my tiny, little rampage is going to make one jot of difference.

Perhaps that's the secret. To just rage on as if doesn't matter, as if nothing matters. Rage, rage, rage. Perhaps that's the insight my daemon was looking for, and it'll leave me alone now. Or perhaps that's a secret it knew all along.

Puppy finishes locking the back seat and I'm vaguely together, breathing better. I might last until I get home. No. I have to go to the university and, FUCK MY LIFE!!!

"So," she says, switching the car on and peering at the screen so she can back along the road, "don't keep me in suspense, bitch! You look all fucked up. What happened?"

My next car will have a reversing camera.

As we roll through the Midlands hills, I fill her in, as much as I can, which is pretty much everything. The cottage in the woods, the dopey detective. I call him that all the way through the story, trying to forget his name. The police station, the cement works. Basically, everything. More than I've told you. About Dan. Some stupid details that seemed important to remember at the time. Dan had more personality than I've allowed, and made a few more jokes, told me more about his life and the army, but it's too painful to write them all down. He was a funny bastard. But still way too dopey to be a good detective.

"Huh. Knew when I didn't get your okay call that something bad happened. Stupid of them to leave your phone on. Made finding you a dodder."

"Doddle."

My correction of her English is automatic, like half my functions at the moment. If I surface from this numbness, let myself feel, I mightblank out and kill her.

Puppy is not her real name. I just call her that, even to her face, because one day she will leave me, too. I am not human. I can't allow my humanity in. I had a dog when I was a kid. It got run over.

I tell her, "It made finding me a doddle."

"Oh, yeah. Doddle." She repeats it a few times, rounding her posh accent to get the pronunciation. We swoop up another hill. I love electric cars for that. No downshift. No noisy engine. No fuss. Just whoosh, up the hill. We're taking back roads, not the motorway. "Doddle, doddle, doddle. I told everyone the Ambassador had an unexpected window to discuss the design with you, so you had to slip away and do that instead. We'll start the interviews tomorrow. Everyone seemed really impressed, and they're all desperate to work with you."

"You're a good puppy, Puppy. You really shouldn't get involved with me. I'm just going to get you killed. You got out. You escaped. You should make something decent with your life."

Puppy snorts in derision. "Bitch, please. If I've learned one thing in my short time here, decent is boring. So, so boring. Security is no reason to kill your dreams."

"Have you been watching the Disney channel again?"

"No! Well, yes, but that's not- It's from some quote I saw on the internet." She frowns at me, puts one hand on my arm, steering carefully with the other. "You might think you're lonely but who the fuck am I going to talk to? When it's late and I can't sleep and the nightmare are in my room and I'm crying. Who else can I call? Not the fucking Ghostbusters. My nightmare are real."

"Nightmares. Plural. Oh, Pups. You shouldn't lean on me. I'm not in control of my life."

"Meh. Who is? So, he's dead? You should say goodbye. You said that yet?"

"No. No, I haven't. Goodbye Detective Dan."

"You named him? Oh, fuck, why did you have to name him? Now you're going to be the one who's all sad and moody. You'll be calling me up at three-thirty in the morning, crying on the phone, and I'll be the one patiently mumbling nice things."

"Just do what I do. Make up a bunch of soundbites and get a computer program to play them at random."

"Ramdom file?"

"Yeah. I just prop the phone up next to the speakers and go rub myself off for ten minutes."

"I'm crying and you play ramdom file?"

"RaNdom fileS. Fuck, bitch. Why am I paying all that money for your elocution lessons?"

"You don't pay. I fucking pay. I stole that fucking money. My money. You're just keeping it for me with your fancy financial hidey thing. Fucking bitch. I pour my heart out and you're off... Digging for clams."

Oh, it's the game. Finding new ways to say dirty things. Shit. What's a good one for masturbation? "Climbing mons veneris."

"Hitch hiking to heaven," Puppy replies.

"Driving Miss Daisy."

"Waxing the carrot."

"Double-clicking the mouse."

"HA!" Puppy laughs. She lost. "That's a good one! Oh, wait, wait. I heard a new one on campus other day. Oh! Yeah, yeah. Riding your rubber bae."

"Rubber bae? Ha! Oh, yes."

"The whole thing is buzzie- No. Buzzing rub. Blah. Buzzing. Rubber. Bae. Too many bs.."

"You need more elocution lessons."

She slowly over enunciates in a perfect Home Counties accent, "Fuck you." Then with different emotional phrasings, "Fuck you. Fuck you? Fuck you. Fuck you... Fuck you. Fuck you. Fuck you!"

We drive a little while and pull over to recharge at some small-town bakery. There's coffee and muffins. Coffee helps. We sit in comfortable silence for a while before we unplug and set off.

Somewhere around Buntingford, she glances across at me breathing and brooding on the passenger seat. "You okay?"

"Bit fucked up, right now, babes. But I'll be all right." I stare out at the sweepingly beautiful countryside. "Besides. Now, I've got all the info I need to finish this."

# 13

# Inn

Birdsong cuts into a dream of my mother with the face of a dog. She's dressed like a serving girl in a Dutch Masters painting, that one pouring milk.

Only my mother-with-the-face-of-a-dog is cutting bread on an old-fashioned, wooden table I vaguely remember from a movie I saw last year.

Even with her tongue lolling out, she still manages to say clear as day, "I'm very disappointed in you, Margaret."

I yell, "Yeah? Well, I'm disappointed you called me Margaret, bitch!"

Then I throw a bloody tampon at her and she scampers away through a giant cat-flap in the back door. Before the flap swings shut, I catch a glimpse of the stars outside. Like the whole house is floating through space. I move over to the curtains, yank them open and the huge sun streams in, suddenly bright, blinding me.

I give a little jerk. My eyes open. The images fade.

Ooof. Not my worst nightmare but...

I'm nauseous. Either from something I ate or from seeing my mother. Dead all these years and she's still in my head. Poor old thing. She never understood, even at the end when it became obvious. Then I realise I'm staring at an unfamiliar ceiling. Wait, where the hell am I?

Fucking shit fuck!

That can only mean one of two things.

There's a distinct, salty smell that tells me exactly what happened. I can barely hold back the rising tears.

Again. I did it again.

Staring at the flecks and variegation in the paint above me, I reach for the glass of water on the bedside table. I always put one there.

As soon as I funnel my lips, I detect the crusty remnants stuck to my face. The residue in my mouth also has a distinct flavour that nearly makes me gag.

I decide I'm not going to blow chunks, and that decision seems to stick.

A slightly bitter taste remains after I wash the furry feeling from my tongue. Hard-water area. Worst thing about travelling away from my little pocket of perfection in Elstead. Fucking hard water. Hate the damned stuff.

The distracting loathing is enough to get my tears in check. The glass clunks back onto the bedside table, muffled by the lace doily thing that makes me think this is a Bed and Breakfast. Finally, I look to my left.

It's not a pretty sight.

Parts of the skull push through the half-eaten face, like a game of peekaboo gone horribly wrong. The nose is missing, making for a curious absence in his profile. From this angle, the exposed teeth make it seem like he's smiling.

I have a flash; something about Hungarians. Was I hungry for a Hungarian? No, wait. Wasn't it the pretty, young woman who was Hungarian? It's all as confused as it usually is.

The shivers hit me. I can't even remember why this poor bastard is dead. Where the fuck am I? How did I get here?

Fuck. This. Shit. Just FUCK IT ALL!

I peer back. There's very little blood on the bedclothes, barely a few spatters on me.

Good. That'll make it seem like the body was killed elsewhere and then moved here. Not something a sweet, weak, little girlie like me could ever do.

If the police even get that far.

Wait. Did I drink the rest? My stomach lurches. Heavily.

Turning from the horror, I take a few breaths, shaking. A scream pushes through. With great effort I manage to contain it to a whimper. Mother-fucking fuck nuggets. This should get easier, but it never does. How many times now? And how long will it take for the itch, the need, to override the revulsion and I start all over again?

Groping blindly for the water, I manage a gulp before the heaving can start. The cool liquid slides down my throat and settles my stomach. I work. I function.

Wait.

What the hell is in my stomach?

*Focus.*

I have to get out of here.

It's hard not to feel a pang of sympathy for him, but a couple of deep breaths and a shake of the head gets rid of that bullshit before it can start in earnest.

Okay.

*Focus.*

I slide from under the covers and slip my feet into my ankleboots. Right where they should be. Huh. I set this place up. That means there'll be notes in my little black book. I should find out who this guy is, and if he gave me anything useful before I ate his… Yes. I ate his face. Fuuuuuuck.

No. Forget that information gathering, cool as practical, fucking bitch. I want to clean this shit off! I hate being covered in other people's bits and blood.

At least my arm isn't trapped underneath this time. Shit, he was a heavy fucker, that one. This one is just kind of pudgy, greying hair, a bit ordinary looking. Apart from the missing chunks of face and the rib-bones showing through the torn-open chest. That's kind of my signature. Still has both his nipples. They actually look kind of big and a bit weird.

I stifle a giggle. Hysteria would be bad right now.

*Focus.*

Got to get going.

It's not dark enough. Too much sunlight through the curtains. The building will be waking up if it's a Bed and Breakfast. There's that whole Breakfast part.

The room is an irregular shape, with exposed beams on the ceiling and walls. Somewhere old then, in that half-timbered style.

Quaint.

I clump over to the little bathroom. The unlaced boots make me walk like a child in grown-up shoes. Quality place. Nice fixtures, tasteful fittings. Pity. The paint needs refreshing. Well, they'll have plenty of opportunity for that, soon.

I do my homework before these things, which hopefully means that diamond-leaded window will drop me somewhere private for my getaway.

There's a noise outside the door. I freeze, naked except for my boots, a bloody, dead mess in the bed and no idea if I put the 'Do not disturb' sign on the door. Feet scuff, floorboards squeak. Another door opens and someone goes inside. A woman giggles.

*Clunk.* I heave a sigh and shuffle over, jamming a chair under the doorknob. That never actually works, but it'll at least slow someone down.

Chair. I touched the chair.

I head back and step into the bathtub, turning on the shower. I fucking hate these shower-in-bath things. Just get rid of the fucking bath. You could make a decent sized shower, instead of being cramped into an awkward space without proper traction.

Wait. Chair, doorknob, shower taps, glass of water.

Remember everything I touched.

I'm still groggy. My head feels like someone's playing a drum on my skull. My kidneys hurt. What's up with that? Like a pain in the lower back but not really muscular, kind of inside. That's the kidneys complaining, little whiners. Protesting about all the salty blood they're having to process.

Yes, little kidneys. I'll try not to do that again.

Anger keeps the tide of sorrow and horror from flooding over me, leaving me sobbing in the bottom of the tub.

I wash my hair, soap the blood off my face, wash my hair again, then do a quick scrub under the fingernails. I collect the facecloth I put over the plughole, wring it out and fold up any stray hairs, pubes, and skin cells inside. Even then, I leave the water running to flush anything I missed.

My best defence at this stage will be to get a long, long way from here as fast as possible. I don't think stray pubes will be my biggest worry. It's a hotel. A lot of people will leave bits of their DNA. They probably won't look too hard for samples, apart from around the body and the bed. Which will be on fire soon.

I stand on my boots as I towel off. Feet have prints, as distinct as hands. Always wear boots. It's not usually an issue, but you never can tell. The cops will keep footprints on record if they get hold of any.

Something nags at me. Something telling me I don't have to worry about that now. Can't remember. It'll be in my notebook.

Clumping back out into the little room with the huge bed, I hunt around with increasing desperation.

Shit.

No clothes!

Shit. Shit. Shit.

I start checking the drawers. Drawer handles, add them to the list of things I've touched. Just some spare sheets and an ugly, patch-crochet throw-rug. No clothes. Nothing.

I have boots, but no clothes?

Fuck. What the hell did I do with them? I get the feeling I did something epic. Like this should be the end, the last, the climax. But it's just some paunchy old dude in a B&B.

What the actual fuck? How can this be the finish? And WHERE ARE MY FUCKING CLOTHES?

O! I want to scream and punch things. And cry. And then faint.

Fuck.

Talk about not leaving evidence. If my bloodied clothes are out there somewhere, I am more than fucked. I'm not even supposed to be alive. Can't let them find something like that.

The shaking starts again and I sit on the bed, trying with limited success to hold back the panic. Desperate thoughts fly around in my head like angry wasps in a jar.

No. Come on. I'm not going to fall apart. I'll think of something. Just follow my protocols.

Wait. How the hell did I get him up to the room? Did people see naked me carrying him through the B&B? Was he alive?

Is this his room?

What the hell happened? Damn.

He's got his pants on, and what's left of a polo shirt that's been clawed to shreds. His sports jacket is on a chair in the corner. How did that get there if he's some pimp? I must have had a big session last night.

Most girls, when they wake up somewhere strange, can just have a cup of coffee and let all the regret come pouring back. I'm going need a fucking séance.

My handbag is tucked under the bedside table. Oh, thank fuck. My nice, big, purple Mandarina Duck. That's some consolation.

There was this one time I woke next to a body and I couldn't find my fucking handbag anywhere! That body didn't even have a head. I had to hunt around in this forest for it. That was a nightmare. Turns out my bag was back in his car.

Wait, wasn't that how all this got started?

Shit.

Handbag, boots, but no clothes? And I made myself a glass of water. And the birds are already chirping. What the actual fuck? My brain is jumping about like a cat chasing one of those little BB8 toys.

Don't get distracted. Procedures. Got to be quick.

I grab a spare sheet and wrap myself toga-style, securing it at my waist with the scarf from my handbag, like a belt. It's a genuine silk scarf. A nice turquoise with some flowers on it. A bit posh, but I like nice things. A quick application of scissors to the crochet-rug and I have a passable hippy-poncho. I take my gloves from the bag and slip them on. Toilet paper to wipe down what I remember touching, and then every other surface. You'd be amazed at the amount of forensic information they can recover from the scene of a fire.

Flush that away, nice and hidden where no cop will ever find it.

Vodka from the bag, and the lighter fluid hidden in the lining. My phone! Oh, my lovely little phone! Along with the gun, notebook, plastic handcuffs, Ziplock bags-

Wait.

I've done this. I've said what's in my bag before. I'm sure this is the end of something, not the beginning. I don't need to list everything again.

Can't get distracted. Shit.

I take a good swig of the vodka then pour in some lighter fluid. Gritting my teeth, I splash some fire-starter on his face, trickle a little into the chest-hole. It rolls off the ribs and splashes down in red. I flinch and have to turn away.

A couple more breaths and I'm okay to finish the narrative. I tip the rest down the back of the bedside table, onto the wall socket. He spilled all down his front, knocked over the bottle as he set it drunkenly on the table. Electrical short.

Yeah, that should do it.

Shit! No! Get his pants off! Dammit, he even has one shoe on, still. Fucking monster couldn't even wait. I throw the pants drunkenly over a chair, wipe the shoe with toilet paper and carefully place it, carelessly discarded across the other. Keep it simple.

I'm about to light it all up when I realise I haven't even checked the fucking window!

I swear to fuck, it's like I want to get caught.

The drop is too far, grass underneath, a little hedged-off back yard with multicoloured bins on a paved section by a door. Not that private. Bad research? Best option? Not my room?

I wipe the window-handle and sill. I probably checked this last night. Better safe, even if I have my gloves on now.

The sun is well and truly peeking. I'll be seen if anyone is looking. Not good. If woke when I usually do, about three to four a.m., there'd be nobody about.

What the hell did I get up to last night?

The vodka/lighter-fluid catches easily and I make sure the fire is well established.

He deserved it. You can bet that anyone my daemon ripped apart definitely deserved it. And the B&B is bound to be insured. It'll be a small fire. There's a fire extinguisher in here. Probably heaps of others in the corridors. They'll be able to keep it contained to this room.

I tuck my gloves back into my handbag, stretch in glorious release, turn and somersault through the window, uncurling gracefully to thump heavily onto the grass.

Oh, the knee loves that. A little tingling up and down my spine, ankles straining, bones jarring. Soooooo fucking glorious! I really should find a way to bottle this and sell it. I'd make a fortune.

A spasm hits and I stagger, feeling the wall slam against my back. I'd have to put on a label, 'May induce unexpected side effects'. My side effect is an image, sharp and sickening. A car on a lonely road.

Ah, that's what his face looked like with a nose. Still not that pretty.

Something dark. A tree. Something very significant about a tree. I'll have to check my notebook.

"Hey. I didn't see you come out."

A tall cutie emerges from the door by the bins, dark hair, little hipster beard. Really nice eyes. Apron.

"No, I've been up for a while," I lie, pushing off the wall and flipping my hair, then I realise I have no wig, no sunglasses. He can see my face! I stare back along the hedge to the car park, like

I'm looking for something. "I came down to have a sly smoke, then realised I don't have any cigarettes. Can I bum one from you?"

"Nah, sorry. I don't smoke. Never have." He leans on the door frame, a little nervous rub of his hands on the apron. Ooo! He likes me!

"Hah! Typical," I say, all casual conversation like. Definitely not panicking about the fire in the room above me. "No-one smokes any-more! Back in my day, everyone smoked, like damned chimneys, all day long."

"Back in your day? What do you mean by that? You look barely twenty."

"Oh, it's just a saying. We had a lot of smokers in my school. Have you started serving breakfast?" A half look back, hand combing my hair, still hiding myself from him. "I'm starving."

"We're just about to," he replies, helpfully hooking a thumb back over his shoulder. "Breakfast is at seven. Do you want me to-" He pauses, sniffing the air.

"You burning the toast or something?" I ask, all sarcastic.

A smoke detector screeches inside.

"Oh, shit," he says. "I think that's a room!"

"Oh, fuck," I reply, covering my face in distress as I peer back at the window I just vacated, smoke puffing out, "Whose room is that? Is anyone in there?"

"Oh, shit. I think I'd better check. What's the fire procedure?" He hurries back inside.

I'm not hungry. I already ate.

Without even bothering to sigh, I stomp off towards the car park, hitching up my toga because it doesn't fit properly.

Fuck this shit. Some pimp in a room. Another fucking fire. I hate that this is something normal in my life. What's *not* normal is the fact that I don't know where my fucking clothes went!

Fuck me dead. This better be some sort of climax. I really want to be able to wake up in my own fucking bed like a normal person, at least for a couple of months in a row. Get some new pottery ideas going.

I'll have stashed my car at a discreet distance. My purple burner phone should have a clue.

Other patrons pour out of the sprawling, half-timbered, whitewashed building, ushered by nervous staff. It's a converted posthouse, doubtless very old, standing alone on the corner of a larger road, and some winding little lane leading up the hill at the rear. The view is very English countryside, if you like that sort of thing.

Which I do.

Open fields, grazing animals, clumps of trees, an early-summer sun peeking over the misty, rolling hills, everything 'so green!' and quiet. Not even that much traffic on the big road. There's a slight chill in the air, but nothing I can't walk off.

I drift casually away.

Smoke belches from the back. I hope next-door got the hell out. The map app finally opens and the GPS has already drawn a line telling me to head, I think, back up the little winding lane.

I'm so anxious to get the hell out of there that I barely remember to walk, not run, and stick close to the hedge. There isn't even a footpath. I'm just traipsing up the narrow byway next to a shallow ditch filled with blossoming cowslips.

And I still have no idea where the flying fuck on a Friday my fucking clothes are.

I remember a long drive, all the way around London, keeping off the motorways and major roads. Buckinghamshire. Is this Buckinghamshire? Took me ages to get here. No, Bucks was the last place, wasn't it? The cottage? Suffolk, then? Am I in Suffolk? Something about a tree.

Ah, fuck it. I'll check the map in a sec, once I've put a bit of distance between me and my latest series of crimes.

After a couple of minutes slogging up this picturesque, twisted little lane, my boots are getting uncomfortable. No socks.

Smoke pours in a healthy pillar from behind the hedge. I can actually hear the faint sounds of fire hungrily devouring the old pub. Shit, is the whole thing going up? Fuck. I only wanted to get rid of any evidence in Faceless' room. Someone was supposed to rush in with a fire extinguisher. Keep it contained. It was probably some sort of listed building.

I am the next wave of destruction for England. Ah, dammit, but I hope everyone got out okay. Did the nice young cook with the very nice eyes go running inside, only to be overcome by smoke and consumed by voracious flames? Can I feel any worse about myself?

I glance down at the phone for a distraction and notice the GPS is telling me that it should take, wait, what? Four point one miles? Fuck! That's not a discreet distance! That's a fucking hike! I stop and stare at my burner like it's telling me it's breaking up with me. That can't be right! Nothing about this is right!

# 14

# Church

A deep panic settles into my gut. The GPS route takes me right through the middle of the village. There are no other roads. I'll be seen for sure.

A hat. Or sunglasses. Something to hide my face. A coat to cover up this glaring fashion-disaster.

I glance back. Smoke billows into the patchy sky among green, rolling idyll. I can't go back and boost a car from the inn. All I can do is clump conspicuously away. Good news, everyone will be staring at the fire.

Oh, fuck, I hope everyone got out all right.

There's a junction at the top of the hill with a little grass triangle in the middle. The new road is not as narrow as the winding lane I just climbed. Opposite the intersection sits a church. Leaning, not chained up mind, just leaning in the gabled porch is a bicycle!

I'm saved! An old-fashioned design with a basket on the front. Nobody stops a bicycle, and it'll take me twenty minutes instead of two hours. Some old dear must be inside doing the flowers. What day of the week is it? Feels like a Thursday. I fucking hate Thursdays.

A couple of seconds waiting, listening attentively, checking the roads. Faint sounds of panic and yelling reach me from the bottom of the hill. I hear nothing else. Not even any sirens. Come on. It's been at least fifteen minutes. Where are the damned fire trucks? We must be a long way from any major town.

Slipping on my gloves, I hitch up the toga and jog lightly across the junction. The lychgate in the low, dry-stone wall is a little to the left. The path then winds past a large beech to the broad porch where my salvation leans.

The chain has a gleam of oil, the tires look pumped and firm. It is a bicycle for which I would happily give my kingdom. If I had one. For a country church, this is large. One hand on the handlebar, I peer inside, wondering if-

"Hello there!"

Shit.

"Um, hi!" I manage, trying for bright and cheerful but crashing into manic along the way.

The middle-aged vicar steps out of the church darkness like Dracula emerging from a tomb. Salt and pepper hair above a lined, homely face. Jeans! Okay, black jeans, but jeans with cargo-pants pockets on the side. A dark, casual jacket. It's only the dog collar and patronising demeanour that give him away.

"Are you all right there, miss?" he asks with an attempt at genuine concern.

"Oh, fine, fine," I answer, twitching my face away from him in a suspicious manner. The accent is slipping into Scottish. You know what that means. Wait, you don't know what that means, do you? How long have you been reading about me?

Damn, but I need this bike.

"I saw you come up the hill from the Lamb," he continues. That cuts down my options immediately. "What's happening down there? Is there a fire? Good grief! You're wearing a sheet!" He steps closer and I curse my luck in finding such a keen observer.

"No, no. It's all fine," I say as causally as my flustered state allows. I try to back away but my heel gets caught up in the damned toga. The nice face has vanished and the priest now wears one of those patentable 'stern vicar' expressions. He grabs my arm.

"I think you'd better come inside and sit down, miss. You might be in shock."

My favourite thing about my handbag is the external pockets. Mostly because they help to break up the shape, concealing what I've done with the lining. I recently had the chance to redo the entire lining so now the external pockets hide handy holes I can reach through to pull out the various, hidden items. It just so happens that right as he says "shock", I fire the taser.

It hits him in the clerical shirt. He makes that hilarious face I always enjoy seeing, then rolls to the floor. The spasms won't last long. I pull out a couple of pairs of zip-tie handcuffs, shuffling one over his shoes to secure the legs. He's recovering when I'm trying to gather his arms, so I zap him again.

The look on his face is priceless.

Then I hear distant sirens and I'm sure the look on my face would be hilarious to someone else. Hopefully, that's the fire engine.

I need to get him out of sight. First, let's stop that stupid mouth. There's a handkerchief in one of his pockets. I stuff that in his gob and look for something to secure it. He struggles, weakly.

Got to get him inside. I don't want to zap him again. He might not survive it. But can I let him live? He's staring at my face, the ordeal etching every detail into his memory. Combined with the description from the cook at the inn, if he didn't rush into the fire, that could undo all my good work at the police headquarters.

Oh, fuck yes! Aylesbury Police Headquarters. I did good work there. Why would I want to forget about that?

I hitch up the toga, grab him with both hands, and drag him down the aisle like a determined bride with a flight-risk groom. He panics, trying to spit out the handkerchief and yell.

Vestry. I'm looking for the vestry. There's a door to the left of the altar, right at the back. My handbag slides off my shoulder, but I let it dangle and haul the thrashing vicar to the secret places of the church.

The handkerchief comes half out and he yells, "Help! Help! Stop this at once! You! Stop this! Help! Somebody help me!"

A kick to the stomach shuts him up a while. Boots are good. Always choose boots.

The fuss and flames should drown out the vicar's cries, even they even make it out of the thick stonework. Something meaningful about church walls muffling the screams of the helpless.

The door is ajar and I bum it open. This is his little office. Sure enough, the narrow window gives him a decent view down to the junction. He saw me acting all suspicious. Fuck.

The sirens seem to have stopped. A rummage through the drawers turns up some masking tape; a lost property box with a pair of bright-green, plastic sunglasses; and a stack of child pornography. Okay, okay, so there's no kiddie porn, but if there were, it might make you more sympathetic towards me for what I'm about to do.

Deep breath.

As I come over to him with the tape he glares. Why is it always so hard to find the start of the tape? The gloves don't help. I get it while he demands with a slight tremble of fear, "What the hell do you think you're doing? Please! Just stop this. You're just upset, in shock."

I kick him in the face. "Shut it! You dinnae have a clue what's really going on," I tell him in my best Scottish accent. Scottish is a great accent for violence. I snatch up the handkerchief and shove it back in. He has a go at my fingers with his teeth, but I've already started with the tape. Practice makes perfect. I don't want to use the duct tape in my bag. It'll make things too obvious.

"I'm no' in shock," I whisper. "You might be, very soon. I cannae have you identifying me. So I'm gonnae take yer eyes."

With my foot, I drag over my handbag. When I snap the knife out of the multi-tool, his eyes go hysterically wide. The thrashing about makes things difficult. I have to put all my weight through one knee into his neck to keep his head relatively still. Even so, I'm not able to cleanly cut his retinas. It takes a couple of tries on his left eye, but the right eye gets completely mashed.

Church walls are great for muffling screams.

I should have that printed on a t-shirt.

He's whimpering and crying through the gag, bleeding tears. I lean down and whisper, "Shhh. Hush now. This is grayte for ye. Now ye spend the rest of yer days martyred as a blind preacher. Well, naer mind tha'. Ye lie there and bleed, like the man next door on the cross. I'm gonna take off ma clothes."

There's a reason I came into the vestry. Vestments. This is where they keep the outfits for the choir, and also where the vicar keeps his dresses. The keys from his pocket unlock a cupboard. It only takes three tries; my hands are barely shaking. Perhaps I am getting used to this. Then I hear more dim sirens, a different tone. Police? I set about in a near-panicked haste.

Bloody gloves will make me look suspicious. Gloves in summer? Ridiculous. Plus the blood. I pull them off. Now, I must remember what I touch.

I untie the scarf-belt, slip off the toga and use it to carefully wipe myself down. There's a mirror in here for the choir to check themselves. A sink with hot water. Bless. I can get properly cleaned and checked.

A red cassock looks enough like a dress, without the white thingy over the top. It even has a little leather belt. I did not know that. Boys large fits well enough. I check my scarf for blood. Nothing stands out. I triangle it and tie it over my hair. The plastic sunglasses don't match, but my identity is hidden and I look much more normal.

Huh. Normal.

I fold the sheet and poncho, which have my DNA all over them, and jam them into my handbag. Using the key in the lock I drag the vestry door closed on the quietly-shifting, blood-weeping priest. He's in shock. I lock the door and walk firmly away.

I don't have anything specific against priests but I'm not exactly a fan, either. Hey. I let him live.

The sun is climbing, though the mist still clings, birds are singing and the view really is very pretty. If you like that sort of thing. Which I do. That's why I live where I live, instead of the bustle of London. Plus, way too many cameras in cities.

A lot of criminals have worked this out, which is why the larger organisations are all moving to the country. That's right, people. An increase of security cameras means the gangs are now invading rural England. The country cops are neither prepared nor equipped to handle it.

My handbag fits neatly into the basket. The GPS is taped onto the handles. It's telling me to turn right, farther away from the fire.

Excellent.

I wheel the bike down the path, almost cheerful. A siren cuts through my mood, wailing closer on the back of a throaty engine.

Shit, it's the fuzz.

We must be near a bigger town for country fuzz to be this close on a weekend. It feels like a weekend. What day is it?

Now, the guilt kicks in, not just for the vicar, but for Headless, The Cottage Crew, poor old Deluded Dan. NO! Fuck. I met him, like, twice. No need to mention his name. I'm going to call him The Dopey Detective. Yeah. That'll help. The Dopey Detective. The Poles at the factory, Watcher, now Faceless. It should be obvious to you that I tend to leave a trail of tears in my wake.

The police car crests the hill and stops at the junction. Using my palms to open the lychgate (GATE!), I exit as nonchalantly as a murdering, eye-carving psychopath. That's a saying, isn't it?

"Miss! Hey there! Miss!"

Wow. It's a woman calling me. Lady fuzz. Wasn't expecting that. Wait. I'm lady fuzz. Aren't I? Something...

Heading vaguely in the direction of the officeress, I reply, over the sound of the siren, "Excuse me?"

The siren derps off.

"Have you seen a woman come up the hill, here? A woman in a poncho?"

"No, I haven't. What's going on at the-" Shit! What did the vicar call it? "-er... at the Lamb?"

"There's been a fire."

"Oh my god! Is that the inn? I thought they were burning hedge-clippings or something!"

"Did you see anyone at all, miss?"

"Is anyone hurt? What happened? How did it start?"

"Miss, could you please help us, here. A woman in a white dress was seen heading up this way. Did you see her?"

"No. I'm sorry, I was in the church doing the flowers. Sorry, was she wearing a poncho or a dress?"

"Both apparently. Do you have any idea where she might have gone?"

"Really? And I thought green sunglasses and my red frock would clash!" She's not in the mood for levity. "Well, I'm heading back to the village, that way. There's nothing down the other way, there, I don't think. Except some old farm buildings."

"Farm buildings?"

"Yes, down on the right, just past thingy's house. Oh, what is that woman's name…?"

"Thank you, miss. You keep safe, now."

The roof lights up, the siren pitches, and the roaring engine drags the fuzz-box away.

Give them something that sounds relevant, and they'll draw their own wrong conclusions.

I stand astride the bike, craning for a view over the hedge, swaying side to side as I desperately try to see what's…

And they're gone.

There probably are some farm buildings down there, somewhere. I used the correct name for the Inn, I knew the way to the village, I just came from somewhere else and had a definite purpose and reason to be there, so obviously I'm a local. It can't possibly be me they're looking for. It might only take a couple of seconds for Lady Fuzz to work it out, or she might not twig until after someone finds the vicar. I'm not taking any chances.

Peddling furiously along the top of the hill, straining the mechanical integrity of the bike, I start to pass a few outlying houses, mostly imitation-stone, commuter mansions. The GPS on my phone says I'm doing fifty-six kilometres per hour. I can peddle faster, but not on this old thing. Okay. About thirty-five miles per hour. I grew up in Australia. Getting sick of these old fashioned measurements.

The road develops stone walls instead of hedges. Speaking of commuters, an early car backs out carelessly and I swerve sharply without slowing, tires complaining at the effort.

The bike is really not used to going this fast.

The clock on my phone is too small and shaking to read. It must be after seven. Why was the vicar in the church this early? Is it Sunday?

There are no cars. Apart from the one that nearly hit me. I brake at a junction, slowing in stages, that smell of burning rubber, and pull over to read my phone. Yep. Sunday the seventeenth, 7:32am. It was a wild Saturday night then. I'll go over my notes in the car, make sense of all this madness.

Starting up, I settle into a more sedate pace, no sirens behind. I barely register the village. A peaceful, curving road beside a low, stone wall protecting a substantial stream that moats the country seat. Houses and adjoining streets opposite the manor house. Kind of a small manor house. The big, country seat is probably somewhere nearby.

A small, council-house estate hides down one road. '50s style, new-brick. The rest of the buildings are old stone, the odd thatched roof here or there, mostly renovated for commuters. I float through a light mist past the village store, Sunday paper headlines gridded behind wire on the sandwich board. I don't want to be Monday's headline, so I stay focussed and peddle up the slight rise. I can't believe I came all the way through here, naked.

The road keeps rising and we leave the village behind, then all my hopes crumble like an Arctic glacier.

I pull over and zoom in on the map, just to be sure.

The GPS is leading me to the middle of that field, there, off that little winding lane, trailing up to what might be a stately home looming behind a gigantic, evergreen hedge. The tippy-toppest windows are visible, so I'm visible from them.

It's the strangest thing.

A big house like this in close proximity to a mark on my GPS. Me with my predilections and habits. It should ring a bell. It should fucking scream at me.

Nothing.

Maybe, once I get past the hedge and see it in all its glory. Well. Let's not get ahead of ourselves. I really don't want to have to go through and clear an entire fucking mansion. Let's remember what's important.

No car.

I'm too disappointed to even swear.

A sigh, drawn out until it hits the muttered curses coming the other way.

Still, I must have marked that spot for a reason. If not, I am so screwed. A quick check over one shoulder and I veer up the lane. Trees meet over the top, dropping the light level. A shiver runs through me. Nothing to do with the weather. There's a kissing gate leading into the first field. I'm so going to have to get rid of these boots. The print will be all over the place.

A cursory wipe of the handlebars and frame, then I dump the bike in a brambly ditch, trusting in the tangle to break up its distinctive lines. Can't leave it in plain sight. No-one will want to go into those thorns after it.

The sheet and poncho make my handbag too unwieldy, so I dump them into the basket. I'll come back for them later.

If there's going to be a later.

That looming house isn't giving me a vibe, but it is giving me the fucking chills. Dominating the skyline, a promise of horror and a seductive calling all at once.

Grazing sheep speckle the second field like congealed mist, still mostly seated and clustered near the water trough.

I slip through the gate. Farther up, towards the massively tall hedge, an indistinct shape sprawls on the ground. Probably just a plastic sheet, or something. Ha. That's funny. It can be seen from the road, but even from where I'm crouching, there's not much to give away the fact that it's a body. Exactly where my GPS is pointing.

How long is this fucking trail of corpses going to be?

Soft mist clings in patches to trees and hedges. I feel like I'm floating in a cloud. The harsh light of day will soon burn the mist away. Can I find the truth in that fading obscurity before I am, myself, revealed? With any luck, the fire will soak up all the local emergency services working on a country Sunday.

The body isn't moving. I'm not exactly concealed in my red cassock against the green hedge. Time pushes me from cautious observation.

I pull on my gloves, trying my best to ignore the damp spot of vicar's blood. Out comes my pistol. The loaded chamber indicator tells me there's already a round in the breech. Did I fire this thing? There is a faint smell about it, but that could be from recent practise.

Crossing directly to the body, I crouch low and press the cold barrel firmly into its ear, something guaranteed to get a reaction from anyone faking.

Nothing.

A little huff of relief. Definitely a dead parrot. He's young, this one. Lithe build. Green, waxed, shooting coat, blue jeans, slip-on boat shoes. He's lying in an awkward mess, bare torso under the jacket. Dressed in haste, then. And shot five times, including once in the leg. The shot's are not clustered. He was moving when he was shot. I slip the extended cartridge out of my FN57 pistol. Holy fuck! Only eight rounds left! I fired twenty-two shots? At what? At whom?

Well, five at him, at least.

I check the other magazine in my bag. Thirty rounds. Not a total bullet-fest, then. I hate having to hunt for spent cartridges. Swapping the full clip into the gun, my gaze follows the slightly obvious track up to a weaker point in the gargantuan hedge.

Right.

Big house it is, then.

Hitching my bag firmly onto my shoulder, I march up to the hedge and press into the gap. A tiny figure in red vanishing into a wall of green.

# 15

# Mansion

This is old. A converted castle, or a fortified abbey. The architecture is twisted with minarets and inappropriate Victorian additions. Two main storeys, windows in the roofs for servants quarters, and probably a cellar underneath. Crenelations all the way around, except for some bits that have balustrades. It's really not that big. Eight, maybe ten bays wide but the 'interesting' architecture makes it loom.

There's a low, hedged section to the right, probably a vegetable patch leading into the kitchen. French windows on the far left reveal the drawing room. The long room in the middle might be a dining room or small ballroom. The beautiful, floral gardens meander to a patio with trellises and more French windows lighting the ballroom.

I can't see what's at the front, but that will be the stables and coach house converted into garages and workshops. I'm sure there's a collection of cars. That'll be telling. If it's all modern supercars, I'll know who I'm dealing with. If it's a bunch of old Subaru Foresters, that'll tell me something else.

It's a very nice house.

Like that place where they shot *To The Manor Born*. Only older. And bigger. And a different architectural style. More of a late-medieval or very early-modern. Okay, so nothing like where they shot that TV series. Do any of you even remember that show?

Why do I bother?

I spy, with my experienced eye, the shrouded tube of a surveillance camera perched in the eaves like a raven determined to nevermore. It's probably quothed something already.

If I was here last night, and I have an increasingly disturbing feeling that I was, then I will be on that footage. But then, if they saw me leave via the hedge, they would have recovered the body from that field.

It all tells a twisted tale of no-one left alive.

I'm going to have to scrub the entire fucking place for fingerprints. Huh. Erasing the security recordings will be a big start. Where's the security office? Or is it all in, like, the study? Or butler's pantry? If this place has the sort of sorry goings on that I suspect, those cameras are definitely not connected to a remote server at some security company. They will handle everything literally in-house.

Private security.

Ex-military private security.

I should be on the lookout for a big, black Range Rover.

An entire palace of death. I'm getting vague memories of running, pursuit, the tree. There was, once upon a time, a very lonely tree. Somewhere. Not here. Everything else is buried in the joy of the daemon. I wonder if 'Ma'am' was in there? Well, let's go and unwrap this little present of mystery.

Pushing from the hedge, I boldly stride through the curved beds of rare roses. A slight rise leads me up to the well-kept croquet lawn. Gorgeous spring flowers in the beds. So beautiful.

No tell-tale flicker of movement from inside.

The French windows of the spacious drawing room at the left are locked. A Yale from last century. Shit, at least give me a challenge. Takes less than a minute to pop. Sometimes, I wish for an audience.

The broad room feels cramped, probably because they squeezed a baby grand into the corner, lid propped open like a dog with its feet on the couch, begging to play.

I resist the urge.

The décor is modernish. Not quite Victorian, and certainly not Art Deco. The couch and armchairs are an updated Chesterfield design that might actually be comfortable. The numerous paintings are all in solid frames, no hint of baroque. That Lucien Freud might be an original. The Caravaggio sketch by the piano certainly is. I'll have that. Petrol money for several years, right there.

As I pass the baby grand, I give in to temptation. It's a Bösendorfer, around one-fifty-five. I lift the fallboard and give it a tinkle. Lovely tone. Slipping my bag to the floor, I pop the pistol onto the top, mildly amusing myself by rotating it so the laser dot aims at some unknown nude's bum. I feel out a couple of chords and have a little riff at the top end. Very nice. Can't be too long, but a little Debussy won't hurt anyone.

"Ah, there you are, ma'am." The voice starts from outside the room, and I snatch up the pistol. "I've done a sweep of the house." He swings through the door. "Everyone else is down-"

I get off two shots before he bolts in panic. Not Bright-Eyes. I think I got him. He's heading for safety, friends, like any wounded animal.

How many friends?

Breathing quickly, I flick my head out and back, checking the corridor, even though I can hear his footsteps pelting away. Corridor's empty, apart from my victim. I scurry after, gun up and ready.

He runs straight past the long dining room and staggers as he fumbles with the kitchen door. Yeah, I got him. This is what happens when you shoot people in real life. Adrenalin kicks in and they can sprint for a good thirty seconds, maybe even a minute before the blood-loss gets them like one too many vodkas.

I love the FN Five-seveN for that. The bullets are designed to penetrate and spurl for maximum internal damage. High velocity, flat trajectory, little recoil. Oh, and thirty rounds in the extended magazines. Love this gun.

The runner is middle-aged, ex-army type in smart casual. He's nothing. It's his "Ma'am" that interests me. The bitch is here! Finally!

Wait, so what the fuck was last night? Who was that guy in the Lamb? And WHERE ARE MY FUCKING CLOTHES?

I reach the kitchen and peer inside, checking the corners, footing the door. The garden entrance is open and I'm a little surprised by that. I thought he was heading for a cellar. That's where they usually hide. Unless he's trying to be sneaky, drawing me to the back door then popping up from somewhere in here.

A check behind the door before I cross over to a window, covering the cupboards, the range. Well, he's hardly going to burst out of the old Aga.

There he is. Outside. One bloody hand on his chest, the other on a cucumber trellis, helping himself along towards... Nowhere? Where the fuck is he going? Towards that shed? Or the mound behind it? It might be an ice-house.

Way back before refrigerators, rich people made little igloos of stone and covered them in insulating turf. Ice inside, and hey!

Cool room for all their perishables. They were usually built out near the vegetable garden. He's not going to reach it.

I push open the window and leap out, tumbling onto the grass and swinging my vision all around, coming up in a ready position.

Nothing.

Shit, that probably looked really impressive as well.

A couple of steps past the trellis and down he goes. Right in the cabbage patch. I stroll back inside and collect my handbag. And that Caravaggio. It nearly fits inside.

Back outside, he's still with the cabbages. I pull out my combat knife. A puzzling thought squints my eyes. Where did I get this? In a forest somewhere. He rolls over, tries a weak move that I'm expecting. I hammer my knife into his temple. Which he wasn't expecting. I wiggle it back and forth and yank it out. He spasms, goes still. The wound spurts, but I'm getting callous in my old age. I am breathing a little oddly as I clean the blade on his Hugo Boss shirt.

There are some hefty, iron keys on an old ring inside his jacket, along with a tall, slim wallet containing over two hundred pounds. Thank you very much. Looks like this is going to be a great haul.

Weeds are taking over the garden. Ma'am probably orders everything from Selfridges and has it delivered. Better security than a prying gardener.

So hard to get good help these days.

The shed is rusted shut and cobwebbed inside. The tools have seen little use. Does she get a service in to maintain the lawns, or do the local Boy Scouts do it for a merit badge?

They have girls in the scouts these days. Interesting times.

A cut in the ice-mound leads to a large, iron door, ajar on a string. Seriously, a piece of green, garden twine is holding the door open. How quaint.

I click on my pistol's tac-light. Now the sun is out and daylight streams through the door, the candles inside provide no illumination of a domed chamber. Not tiled in red. Cramped. Barely enough room for one person to stand inside and access the shelving, which is no longer there.

A broad well sinks into the opposite side. The lid is propped nearby, revealing a spiral staircase descending into darkness.

Okay. That's creepy.

There's something about this whole place that's raising hackles. Maybe all the killing and mutilation is catching up with me. Finally.

Another candle flickers below. There are other candles, but they're all burned down. No-one replaced them since last night.

The stone steps are beyond ancient, worn almost to a slope in the middle. Centuries old. Was the well built next to the abbey, or the other way around? Water drips somewhere below. Perfect. All I need is a hooting owl and someone playing long, drawn-out violin couplets.

Okay. I guess I have to go down.

Oh, shit, I've got to wipe the piano before I leave.

And the window handle in the kitchen.

No, wait. Gloves. I'm literally looking at my hands encased in fucking gloves. What the fuck is wrong with me?

Take your time answering.

I slip the sunglasses into a corner of my handbag. My boots get good traction. The descent is a long one, three or four storeys worth.

Around and around, down and down.

No. This can't be right, can it?

I was blindfolded way back when I was made. Yet this feels so familiar. My daemon squirms, flushing me with sensation. I breathe.

*Focus.*

Stagger and slip.

I reach for the pillar on the inside of the spiral staircase, feet grabbing for the outside, where the stairs are wider, where I feel more stable.

That stability doesn't come.

Is this it? Have I found them at last? That bitch from the ritual? I have her face burned into my brain.

I stand there, grasping the walls, legs shaking, trying not to get too excited. I should just head down. Find out. I'll know if I reach the red room.

I feel steadier once I start down. At the bottom is an antechamber with an early medieval feel about it. Irregular stones with recently re-pointed mortar. Air blows in from some rusty vent. A row of modern hooks is bolted to the wall with an assortment of posh clothing. Male and female.

I'll go through the pockets for change later.

The bench is no more than twenty years old. Not a red chamber. A camera peers down from the ceiling. I didn't see any upstairs, and no cables, either. The cable from this one leads along the arched stone corridor. No point in creeping. They know I'm coming. I try some calming breaths, long and slow.

Nope. Not helping.

I walk strongly down the corridor. Maybe definite movement will get my quivering insides under control. Handbag hitched tightly, gun low in a firm Weaver grip, and something damaging my calm.

There's a distinct change in the corridor. Larger, regular stones tightly fitted. Blue granite all from the same quarry.

Roman? Fuck me, how old is this place? The Romans were in England for almost four centuries. Plenty of time to build whatever the fuck they wanted.

My legs are jelly. Is this what it's like to be a normal person? I haven't been one since the knife. Or has my daemon left me? Am I just a weak, pathetic girl again?

My shoulder hits the wall of the corridor, and I realise I've staggered. Eyes leaking, I lean heavily, knees barely able to hold me upright.

I can hear voices now. Can't make out what they're saying. A low, male voice, deferential to the aristocratic female.

Ma'am.

Holy shit! Am I finally going to meet The Lady herself? A flush of energy rushes through me from that thought. I walk on, blood pounding in my veins.

How can there be blood pounding in my veins? That should be impossible.

A chamber opens to one side with two ante-chambers on the other.

Oh shit.

"Try zooming in or something," The Lady says.

"Yes, ma'am."

The chamber is my own personal hell. A vaulted, Roman bellpit coal mine, backfilled with stonework, mosaic frescoes all the way up the three-storey, domed ceiling. Red and flames and monsters. A place built by some local Roman deviants to worship Hades in his underworld aspect. Pluto. The Romans called him Pluto.

A stone altar sits in the middle, a row of robed bodies laid out respectfully by the entrance. Neatly arranged. There's a small pile of bullet casings. Twenty-two of them.

I recognise one of the corpses and almost lose myself to the daemon in ecstasy.

With effort, I keep it at bay, hovering there, tasting the excitement and horror coursing through me.

This is where I was made. They had a hood over my head when they brought me here, and I was dead when they took me out, so I didn't recognise anything upstairs. But this, I know. The particular red of the tiles, robed figures around me.

"Can you read her lips? What the hell is the little cunt saying to him?"

There's nothing quite so amusing as a really posh person swearing in clearly enunciated profanities. I suppose everyone's human. To an extent.

"I'm sorry, ma'am. I've got the volume all the way up, but it's distorting."

The air-circulation pump hums quietly, not really covering the sound of my footsteps.

"What about from this angle, up here? Can we see what she's doing with his hand?"

"That's even farther away, ma'am."

"Dammit! I just want to know what that bitch is saying to my father!"

They didn't see me coming on the cameras because they are admiring the recording of my handiwork from last night. If they heard me they must have assumed I was the cabbage-patch kid.

I'm trembling in earnest.

"Do you want to know what I said to him?" I ask, voice shaking with excitement and fury as I step into the ante-chamber's doorway.

I shoot the bald-headed hard-man twice in the chest. Only, the first shot cracks his sternum and he flinches so violently that second shot skims past his shoulder, breaking one of the four monitors sitting on the wooden table.

They record the ceremonies they perform, probably for blackmail purposes.

I wait for him to gasp and collapse before carefully placing the little red dot on his head and squeezing, not pulling, the trigger.

Blood splashes in red, coating the wall behind.

Ah, yes. It's all coming back to me. The old woman starts to rise, then starts to sit, then hovers half-way, hands wandering nervously. The other guard, who thinks he's sneaking up behind me, swings something that cracks hard across the back of my skull.

On anyone else, that might have been a fracture, concussion, game over. The daemon revels in the sensation.

I turn back with an evil look. It's Bright-Eyes! "Hello, old chap," I say. He stares at me in awe. No doubt wondering why I'm not lying on the floor at his feet. Then it hits him. The bright eyes register my face and I see that familiar look of astonishment.

"You? The fucking potter? How the hell can it be you?"

They didn't know! Ha! I thought they practically had me, and they weren't even close! Oh, that's just hilarious.

"I've brought you a message," I tell him. "Detective Ripplewater is waiting for you."

To his credit, Bright-Eyes only blinks once before snarling and swinging the flashlight at my temple. I slip under and swing for his ribs.

He's fast, though. He pulses back with a boxer's instincts the moment I start ducking, so I just graze him.

My abused head complains at my sudden motion. I surf the spike it gives me, and come back upright, turning for a back kick.

I never really learned how to control the daemon until I took up surfing when I was in Australia. The second time. I let the feelings crash through me, and I ride my focus down, keeping just enough control. Maybe a little wobble.

Bright-Eyes gives me a confused look as I my foot speeds through the air at his face. He uses the torch to smash it aside at the last second, stumbling back, swinging the return at me as I land. The blow catches me in the side of my protectively-hunched shoulder.

Ow.

The fucker is good.

Levels. Never stay at the same height. I roll down, leaning back. The soldier plants his foot and swings the torch like a club at a baby seal.

Oh, how sweet. He thinks he has a chance against me.

Punching down hard, I shatter his foot, keeping close as he staggers, screaming. Stepping firmly, I spike my elbow into his nose. There's a sickening crunch. His head snaps back, lifting him and laying him out a good half a body length away.

Not bad for an eighteen-year-old girl. Although, I have been eighteen for a many, many years.

The long, heavy-duty flashlight rolls from his fingers. Yeah, could have hurt someone with that.

I pick it up as he twitches on the flagstones trying to work out why he's looking at the ceiling. That ceiling is a view I remember all too well. I shoot him twice in the head and turn back to the security alcove.

The woman found her guard's automatic and opens fire. Oh, fuck, I hate guns. So hard to keep control. And they leave horrible marks that take ages to fade.

Two of the six shots hit.

Terrible grouping.

One hits me just above my right hip. I wince as my control slips. The other shot catches my left arm. More of a glancing thing, but still really painful.

I nearly vanish into the daemon's ecstasy, floating above the scene. But I know who this bitch is, and it's important. I fly on this feeling, still with enough of a connection to say, "Forty-five calibre. Excessive. 1911. Only six shots. Must be an older model."

She clicks the trigger a few times in desperation.

I tell her, "Bullets always leave nasty bruises on me. I'm not entirely sure how."

My red dot flows and I take out her left kneecap. She screams in a way that is familiar to me.

I wasn't running from that dead man in the field. He was fleeing me. That was as far as he got before the adrenalin failed, blood-loss laying him down to sleep. He was the one who was going to rape me.

Ma'am slides down the wall, still screaming. I give her time to sob and cough in agony. There's a rhythm to these things.

Ambling over, I crouch. Each movement a vibration in ecstasy that threatens to send me swimming into the stars. I let the Mandarina Duck slide to the floor, flick my safety on with my forefinger and toss the FN FiveseveN onto the table.

"It's a complete mystery to me how my body works," I say to The Lady. "How I get bruised. Why the bruises fade. Why I panic and swim with adrenaline, how my blood pumps faster in moments of joy and terror." She's present enough to register what I'm saying through her pain. Tough old bird. "Let me show you the cause of my dilemma." I untie the headscarf, undo the belt and lift the holy (and holey) cassock off, naked except for my boots.

I peel off the medical strip.

Gently lifting her fingers to the line under my left breast, pushing the skin apart, I slide her entire hand inside me. Under and around the ribcage we go. Quite the journey.

Eyes wide, she starts crying in confusion and agony.

"Can you feel my right lung, there?" I take a slow, deep breath. "Yes? And my left lung over on that side?" Breath. "And at the back, in the middle? That cavity? That space?"

The realisation creeps in, sobering her, blanking her own pain as she remembers my features, eyes flicking to the monitor where I'm doing the same thing with her father's ancient hand, on a loop.

"That's where you cut out my heart. In that very chamber. Over there. I don't know how the blood flows through my body with no heart to pump it. I don't know how I work. But I do. I eat and shit and sweat and sleep and fuck and breathe. My hair and nails continue to grow. All with an absence in my chest. But I don't age, get sick or injured. You know, I twisted my knee at hockey practice a couple of weeks before, and it was mostly better, but it's not fully healed to this day. It's better than it was, but it still aches, *aches* in the cold. I'm not quite frozen in time, but somehow, I don't change." I glance at the monitors. "Your father was young when he took my heart and fed it to you."

"Oh, god, no!"

"And you. You. You were barely my age, weren't you? I hunted for you. It took me a while to work it out, but you were at that party in college, weren't you? Even though you didn't go to school there. Talking to me, my friends. Learning that my father was dead and I'd already tried to run away from my mother. Learning that

I was some poor man's daughter. A man who climbed and earned his position in his company. A man who spent much of his salary on his daughter's private education. You thought I didn't belong, so no-one would miss me."

"Margaret? Oh, god! Margaret..."

"Ideal for your sick purposes. I remember the ceremony, that special role you had to perform. But I'd seen you before then, hadn't I? Out looking for victims. And you found me. My daddy left, abandoned us so we wouldn't have to watch him die of lung cancer. I went a bit wild, rebellious. Potential runaway, missing person. So you lured me here for your pathetic, useless ritual."

"Useless? It worked! You haven't aged a day, Margaret! You can be the one to teach us! Teach us all! Tell me, please! By all the gods, tell me! How did you become this vessel?"

"How did I become like this?" I grip her wrist tightly, lean in. "I died. You killed me."

"So we summoned the Lord of-" I slap her face.

"No! You didn't summon anything!"

Gently, I remove her hand while she stares, shock, horror, pain and confusion in the aged lines of her face. I feel the texture of her skin against the edge of the cut, the texture of her knuckles, finger-joints all swollen with arthritic age, sliding out of a wound that is still fresh but never bleeds. Still tender, sometimes sharply so. A hole that leads to the emptiness within.

"Do you know how to get rid of warts, little girl?" I ask her. "There are hundreds of old-wives recipes. Do you know why? Because some warts eventually go away of their own accord. Whatever method the patient happened to be using when the wart disappeared, that's the cure they write down."

"What does that have to...?"

"There are beings in this universe we could not hope to understand any more than an ant could understand a mobile phone. Larger than planets and mostly incorporeal, they swim in suns and delight at the sensation. They spend aeons drifting between the stars, revelling in unknown radiations. Sometimes, an aspect of them will drift through a planet, and they will leave a part behind to swim in the heat and cold and layers of the world. On that night, an aspect of one drifted through me in a moment of such intense emotion. Like poor old Vlad in his utmost despair, ambushed and slaughtered by his own troops. It's a shame you'll never meet old Vlad. He's a nice man. Sells insurance."

"Insurance? What is...? Sun?"

"These sun-swimmers will leave an aspect of themselves to swim inside a person, feeding back those bizarre, incomprehensible emotions, unique sensations unavailable anywhere else in the universe, to a host who might be a thousand light-years away and barely registers it. When that happens, when that connection is made to the sun-swimmer, whatever meaningless ceremony you pathetic cultists happen to be performing, for whatever god you have invented, you write that down as a way to summon a daemon. You don't summon a creature like that. You don't get one inside you with some silly ceremony. You have to actually suffer. Horrifically. And then die. Even then it's one in several billion. You're not prepared to suffer and die on that tiniest off-chance, are you? You want what your kind always wants. All the benefits with none of the work."

"I- I would. I would try anything. To have what you have."

"What I have? The fuck do you know about what I have? When we connect, the sun-swimmer and I... O! you have no idea what I can feel!" My fists ball up in her tweed jacket, lift her half a metre of the floor. "You give them pointless titles, invent spheres of influence, and tell yourselves you can ask them *favours.Control* them, if you speak in Latin or Urdu or some other nonsense. They don't even know you *exist*!"

I set her back down. She writhes on her shattered knee.

"When I woke up all those years ago in the back of that car, wrapped in a blanket, ready to be dropped into the ocean. When I woke up and tore that man's head clean off, then climbed from the wreckage without a scratch, I caught a glimmer of this, the merest hint of what it's like to bathe in the stars!"

I'm floating further, connecting to my daemon, sipping the tiniest hint of what my sun-swimmer is feeling.

Oh, fuck! You have no idea!

"For years I didn't understand. I tried to live, tried to die. Tried every drug and experience under the sun and the moon. Then I saw him. That man. The other one whose face was uncovered."

"There was no-one! They all wear the robes. We always- So no-one knows."

"Oh, there was one. Think."

"Oh. Oh, no."

"I followed him down to the river, trying to decide if it was him. Trying to decide what to do. And I was clumsy about it. And he saw me. Then there it was. It was all there, just that one thing I can see in your eyes. A little spark of recognition. He knew me. He knew what he'd done, that man."

"Oh, please, no!"

"Who squatted over me that night, feasting on the other side of my heart while he fucked you."

"No, no, no. That wasn't me. That was a lifetime ago!"

"You both fucked and ate my still-warm heart as I bled to death beneath you! And a bunch of sad men in silly costumes stood around and masturbated. I found him. Oh, yes. That wasn't a boating accident that killed little Lord Twatface. That was an ecstasy I'd never felt before.

"And now I can't stop myself. Hunting you people down, your little cabals. All the others who play at being evil because they think it makes them special. They don't want to fuck you anymore, do they? So, what? You supply them with girls? Ah, that's it, isn't it? You're just another pimp. And I get to do horrible, horrible things to you and lose my mind in ecstasy. All you little cunts, all over the world, tearing you apart. Wait. Who the fuck was that guy back at the bed and breakfast?"

"What? What the hell are you saying? You're not making any sense! This is all just nonsense! I don't do anything. They blackmail me to get access to the house. My father! Oh, my father! You? What did you do to him? NO! This isn't right! This isn't right!"

I stare down at her. She's in denial. What a sad way to go.

"Is this nonsense, little girl?" I bellow as I rip her arm from its socket, beating her about the head with it. "Is this not right?"

Then the daemon takes me.

# 16

# Estate

Watching their security feeds helps fill in the blanks. I waited a couple of days after they killed The Dopey Detective. I won't name him. It makes things easier. I changed my hair colour, different make-up, darker lippy, a bit heavier around the eyes. That's about all the disguise a woman really needs. Men are that shallow. No, seriously.

I pretended to be a runaway, came onto their radar through the Birmingham circle, went to the old tree like they told me. I was expecting just one of them but they were desperate to catch the planetary alignment. Like the position of a few motes of dust actually matters to a sun-swimmer half a galaxy away.

They 'captured' me, took me to that Roman hell. I recognised it, my red pit beneath the earth, where they chained me down and cut my clothes off. The old man was there. He recognised me, eventually, after I snapped my chains, shot most of his friends, had my fun with the rest, and showed him where my heart should be.

I was so happy! Filled with indescribable joy at finally having my revenge. So happy. Because of that, the daemon didn't properly fade like it usually does. It lingered, enjoying the emotion, feeding it, feeding off it.

I knew one had escaped.

Because I was going outside, I put my boots on. Because I might need a new clip for my gun, I picked up my handbag. Then I walked away, naked, shooting that wounded straggler cowering behind the shed. He tried to flee. Didn't make it far. Just to the middle of that field.

I saw a car coming along the bottom of the hill, marked the position of the body on my GPS. Some part of me, somewhere inside, knew I was going to have to deal with that. Still swimming with my daemon, I ran down to meet the late-night driver.

I wanted to celebrate.

Just some ordinary, passing schmoe. Travelling salesman. He stopped, offered me a lift, offered his jacket to cover my nakedness, snuck me up to his room at the B&B. I showered, set the room then threw him onto the bed, which, from the look on his face, he was half-expecting. He was not expecting me to jump on top, spear my hand into his chest and pull open his ribcage, choking him with my other hand so he couldn't scream as I sank my teeth into face.

Ah fuck.

As my stomach heaves, the memory slides. I pull over, open the car door and throw up. Chunder. The vomit is tinged red. Be thankful you'll never see that colour in your own vomit. It's not conducive to a calm, sane demeanour.

Duffy is begging me for Mercy! Mercy! from the radio.

I take a few breaths while leaning out of the inevitable green Subaru. British racing green. Fucking hideous colour for a car.

There was a beautiful old Austin Healy 3000 in the garage. Powder blue top, cream along the sides. A white Volvo XC60, the mid-size, not the full XC90, which Ma'am and her boys arrived in. Under a tarp, she had an older Aston Martin but, like, one from the '80s or something. Not one of the cool ones. I think her dad brought it and kept it here. Too old to drive any more. Fucker must have been in his nineties. Did he live here? No idea.

The folks for the ceremony arrived in a glorious collection of very bog-standard vehicles. Old money seldom drives show-off cars. Two Toyotas, an older Lexus, an Audi. One electric car. A Polestar. Okay, a couple of beamers, but not even the seven series. Fives or threes. None of them black.

I wonder what happened to the black Range Rover?

Antonio is going to have an elegant Italian conniption when I tell him I took the inconspicuous Outback. He loves those old, '60s sports cars, Austin Healys, Triumph Spitfires, Alfa Spiders. The thought of missing out on an Aston Martin will kill him.

I don't have the same nostalgia for old things. History is mostly pain for me.

I grabbed the Subaru Estate because I wanted to nick a couple of things. I hid a few selected paintings, a nice vase or two, and a little Georgian side table that I think might be a William Moore, all under some blankets in the back.

"Mercy! Mercy!" sings Duffy.

I have no mercy. I'm not going to stop. I can't. I'll have a little break, a few months, get that commission done for the Swiss Ambassador. That was genuine, as well as a cover. I'll fence this lot and that will pay for a move and name change.

But the itch will be back soon enough. Even my revenge won't stop that. You think drug addicts have it bad? There is nothing, literally nothing on this Earth, oh, baby.

Ah, fuck it. I spit out the last of the red vomit and slam the door. Throttling up, I drive on down the road.

So, Faceless, the dude I burned at the Lamb, was just some helpful passing motorist. A nice guy. I tore him apart and drank his blood because I was feeling really good, and the daemon doesn't know any other way to celebrate. I can remember my teeth scraping along his skull as the flesh tore free.

Well, can't be helped.

Fuck! I have got to stop saying 'well' at the start of all my sentences!

A good swig of Remy Martin Cognac washes away the bad taste. Nice liquor cabinet. I suspect she drinks to forget, and can afford to do it in style.

Drank. Past tense.

I feel the warmth and the edge of a buzz half a bottle will bring. How does that happen? How do I process it? How can I get drunk? Why does it take so damn long? How does my blood still flow? From where? To where?

I collected the body in the field. The sheet and poncho were still with the bicycle. Did you forget about those? I nearly did. The house security room was easy to find. Butler's pantry. I destroyed the hard-drives from there as well as those from the bell-pit, checked there were no back-up servers.

Don't worry, I wore my gloves the whole time.

In any case, I think this might get flagged for the attention of one Tracy Wendover, who will leave her fingerprints all over the place, just in case.

The old woman had a good collection of slacks and blouses. A couple fit okay. Yes, I'm wearing dead, old-person clothes. I turned up the circulation pumps and burned the ice-house, piling the cassocks and everything into a nice bonfire in the well-ventilated ante-chamber. They'll find the chambers, the bodies, the altar, all in ashes, and probably cover it up, or maybe clean it out and open it to the public.

The archaeologists will want a look first.

Will they connect it to the fire at the Lamb? Probably. I heard later that they managed to save the old inn. It was just a couple of rooms and a lot of the thatch.

They'll have a fun old time trying to work out how my last victim fits into it all. One more to add to my ever-growing list of unjustifiable cruelties. I leave a trail of calamity and carcasses wherever I go.

I ate an innocent man's face. You think that should make me feel a particular way, but it doesn't. I am, after all, a heartless woman.

# Acknowledgements

I'd like to take the opportunity to thank all my friends for their support.

Other titles by this Author:

Cruel Provocations

Coming Soon:

Desolation

Milton Keynes UK
Ingram Content Group UK Ltd.
UKHW020241201124
451446UK00009B/121

9 780975 613832